D0571617

THE TIME OF THE TEXAN

In the Old West, the peril to South Texas from Mexican marauders was a constant danger. Men retired for the night with the knowledge that next day they might arise robbed of their livestock, left destitute, or having to dig graves for their neighbours.

The Mexicans never forgave Texans for rebelling against Mexico and establishing a republic of Texas or for joining the United States.

Texans and Mexican bandits met in battle, two national boundaries were violated, men killed, and blood shed in South Texas...

THE TIME OF THE TEXAN

Lauran Paine

GUNSMOKE

First published by John Gresham, Ltd.

This hardback edition 2003
by BBC Audiobooks Ltd
by arrangement with
Golden West Literary Agency

ISBN 0 7540 8248 2

British Library Cataloguing in Publication Data available.

Printed and bound in Great Britain by
Antony Rowe Ltd., Chippenham, Wiltshire

Chapter One

THERE WAS SIMPLICITY to the smell of sweat and the grumbling of men's voices. There was inexplicable promise in the far night sky and the way its stars caught at a man's mind cradling it with a kind of timeless promise.

There was also, at the end of each day, a time when no spoken word was important regardless of the seeming urgency that lay behind its utterance, and as the Texan lay there feeling ancient kinship with the dust, the sweat, and the far sky, he closed his mind against the sounds around him; let his body run fully loose against the ground. He considered again the things Florence had said before he had led out this posse and as always, his conclusions remained unaltered.

This was his kind of life, this lying upon a salt-stiff saddle-blanket with others of his kind close by in the night. A man, he felt, was meant to be part of this kind of life; he was born to peril and hardship, and if he found pleasure after long intervals of labour this made the pleasure and the solace more precious to him, and it also made the things men valued most, and the reasons they tried to achieve them, vary greatly. There was for example no pleasure money could equal nor any words which could adequately describe, the first drink of cold spring water after a long hot day in the saddle.

There was no comparable sensation, he thought, to stretching out upon pine-scented ground on a summer night after gruelling hours of hard riding; of feeling one's body go loose in every joint and muscle.

It was the little things : the hard bite of aromatic tobacco after days without a smoke, the comradeship of quiet good men, the look of night-sky beyond tips of pine trees, its hush, its timelessness, its promise. These were the things which made life worth living to Westerners—but how did one explain them to a woman like Florence Berry whose entire background was so different?

He did not know; he knew that he lacked the articulate ability to do so and this was a frustrating sharp pain in him. How did you convince a woman who hated guns and dust and a faded sky that each was a segment of the West—that without the guns there could be no safety for one's children; without the dust and the heat there could be no West at all, and that what he believed in was simply that by facing these things, by forcing them into orderliness, the West had a future while without facing them, or by running from them, it had none.

He remembered the tilt of Florence's head as she had watched him ride out of town with the posse. He remembered her moments of long silence when they had been together and wondered now at the secret things behind those silences.

She was a full woman; he had often seen in her eyes that depth of knowledge that revealed how well she knew what life really was—and what she was convinced it ought to be. The things she had said came now across the space which separated them to touch him.

" ' Clint; you surely want more than this . . .'." Sweeping one hand eloquently to include the wide dirty street of Travis, Texas; its rows of stores and saloons, livery stables, banks, bakeries and cafés. " ' You can't be content with this '."

He remembered sitting mute that time, considering the little cow-town, thinking his thoughts and saying nothing; searching for a way to put intuitive feeling into words, and failing.

He remembered other meetings also. Two days earlier, when he had ridden out of Travis with the posse, she had said : " ' All you have to do is let the Army know. That's why it's out here, Clint—to apprehend and punish outlaws and brigands '."

Those were the painful things Clint Verrill remembered now, with his body at peace and that high vault of heaven bringing solace to him from beyond tree-tops.

He also remembered her black hair let loose around the beauty of her face, the symmetry of her features and the deep, violet blueness of her eyes. It was with those thoughts and memories uppermost, both poignant and hungry, that he fell asleep, and they were still in his mind when he was awakened in the pleasant chill of pre-dawn.

"Hey, Clint; you going to sleep all day?"

It was tough Johnny Welker, wiry-thin and as durable as rawhide. Like all itinerant cowboys Johnny was indeterminately youthful in a way common to Westerners; he was young in years but old in spirit and wisely experienced in fatalistic acceptance; Johnny Welker had killed men; he would kill still other men, but like the others around Clint now in that grey, uncertain light, he smiled easily and joked often because he had long since rationalised that continued survival—all that really mattered—required killing. It was not a sin, it was a necessity. He stood there now, lean face whisker-shadowed, watching Clint stir to life, and he said : "Well; when a feller's got a clear conscience he gets to sleep early and he wakes up early."

There was a mocking, faint look of amusement in his gaze. Like the others, he knew Clint was having a hard time of it with the girl from the East.

"Are the horses saddled?" asked Clint, getting stiffly upright and gazing over where fifteen hunkering, mumbling shapes were poking at a little fire and drinking coffee.

"An hour ago," Johnny replied. "Come on. Those Mexicans won't be sittin' around waiting for us."

Clint stepped into his boots, pulled on his hat, buckled on his gun and shell-belt one-handed and started forward. Someone offered him a tin cup of scalding coffee. He drank it and made a face.

" Strong enough to melt a brass monkey," he said.

" Naturally," said Carl Benton, the town black-smith, dryly. " We tell when it's boiled enough by throwing in a horseshoe. If it sinks it ain't—if it floats it's ready to be drunk."

The men smiled. Carl Benton was a saturnine, massively muscled squat man who always wore, in church or at work, a very impressive gold watch-chain across his leather vest. One end was connected to a big gold watch, the other end was attached to a small Comanche ' pukutsi ' charm. Carl, one of the oldest men in the posse, had been an Indian fighter in the early days; he did not ordinarily say much. He had a way of squatting in the dust and fixing slitted eyes on something far off for sometimes a full minute before he spoke. He never moved nor spoke hurriedly and because of this and the fact that he was wise in the ways of outlaws and marauders he was greatly respec-ted.

" I made a little scout," Carl said now, looking into his tin cup, sloshing the gritty dark contents. " I come to some conclusions."

" Such as?"

" For one thing, those raiders outnumber us about two-to-one."

" I figured that," Clint said, squatting. " Any time Mex cattle thieves come raiding up into Texas they like to have plenty of company. What else?"

" They don't know the country very well."

" No?"

"Nope. They're driving the stolen critters straight for Chavez Ravine."

This pronouncement held the possemen thoughtfully silent for some time. Chavez Ravine, named after a long-defunct Mexican raider, bisected the prairie for fully three miles. It was one of these idiosyncrasies of Nature for which no acceptable explanation had been offered; for no apparent reason at all in the middle of an endless Texas prairie, Chavez Ravine cut a half mile wide gash running almost three miles east and west. It was quite deep, had a tiny creek meandering along its floor, and from the prairie itself those unfamiliar with the area had no warning whatsoever that it was there until they came upon the sheer dropoff. There were several game trails leading down through sagebrush to the willow-lined bank of the small creek, and the age of Chavez Ravine could at least be guessed at by the fact that some enormous black-oak trees grew there, and as every Westerner knew black-oaks were the slowest growing trees in the country. Legend had it that, aside from the Mexican marauder for whom the ravine had been named, it had harboured hostile Indians, Texan desperadoes, killers on the run and every variety of outlaw imaginable since the first white men found it. It's evil reputation, now, caused Clint Verrill's possemen to look grave. One of them, young and newly-married Foster Gorman, broke the long silence with a question.

"Don't you figure they'll have an outrider on ahead, Carl, and that he'll see it?"

The blacksmith wagged his head, still inspecting the

myriad coffee grounds in his cup. " Figure not, kid," he replied with a minimum of words. " When I left their trail and started back for camp here, they was already too close to cut around either end of the Ravine without a heap of unnecessary riding." Benton raised his head and threw a saturnine look at Sheriff Verrill. " Do you read anythin' in that, Clint?"

Verrill finished his coffee before answering. " Kind of early in the morning for being clever," he said, knowing very well that Benton had a theory and wanted to expound it.

" Well; I been awake longer," retorted the blacksmith. " I think, since they come up out o' Mexico in the night and bore east toward the cow country around Travis, that they missed the thing altogether, you see, and now, still not knowin' it's there, they've rid plumb into it."

" And?"

" And about this minute they'll be laughin' and jokin' about their good luck in findin' it, and'll be pushin' the cattle down there thinkin' that no posse'll find them because they'll be hid."

" I see. You think they just might stay down in there to rest their animals."

" Yup. Maybe until nightfall, Clint."

" In that case," Johnny Welker exclaimed, making a cigarette, " we'd best be getting along so's we can kind of disillusion them while it's still daylight."

They all arose, emptied their cups and started for the horses. Clint hung back; the matter of approaching the Ravine was troubling him. Perhaps the Mexican rustlers thought they were safe as Benton said, but strangers to Texas or not they would have at least one sentinel watching their backtrail. He could not hope to lead fifteen men across a flat, treeless, brushless South Texas prairie very far before he was seen, and thirty or forty armed, desperate Mexican gunmen, were not likely to abandon their stolen cattle and flee from half as many Texans.

" Come on," Welker called from the saddle. " Doggone, Clint; it takes you longer to wake up than any man I ever seen." Johnny, garrulous as usual, sounded now just a little annoyed as well.

They left the pines and struck out over the plain. At Bajain Wells, a series of mud-bottomed buffalo wallows, they halted to water their horses. Beyond, they followed some broken, slight rises in the terrain as long as they could then left them riding south. From here on there was no cover for a hundred miles, not even sagebrush.

Riding stirrup Carl Benton said to Clint. " Wish we'd known this last night. Only way to slip up on those devils is in darkness."

Clint made a cigarette and lit it before he replied. " Last night you couldn't have tracked them, Carl. Besides, we wouldn't have known they were going to Chavez Ravine."

The sound logic of this statement did nothing to abate Benton's worry. He continued to squint far ahead and mutter to himself from time to time.

Behind them came the others, mostly silent, a few smoking, some restlessly anticipating a hard fight and therefore grim in the face. Johnny Welker was the only man among them who rode easy in the saddle humming to himself, slack-bodied and unconcerned.

"Maybe," Carl finally ventured, "we'd ought to wait till night, Clint."

"I thought of that. The trouble is, they'll likely get away in the dark."

"Probably. But we'd recover the cattle."

"Maybe, Carl, but if we didn't it'd be pretty hard to explain how we lost both the critters and the rustlers too."

Benton subsided. They rode on for another half hour then daylight came with the suddenness which characterised sunrise in South Texas. One minute they were riding along through murk and grass shadow and the next minute an enormous yellow disc popped up over the rim of the world and dumped hard yellow light over everything.

"And that," Johnny Welker sang out with finality, "is that." He meant they would now be visible and he was correct.

Clint halted when they could distantly discern the Chavez Ravine area far ahead. He had made up his mind and while his plan was actually nothing more than a pell-mell charge, which he hoped would enable them to at least get within rifle-shot before the rustlers saw them and fled, he was not very hopeful.

"Carl; take half the men and circle around to the east. The rest of us'll stay here until we figure you're about even with the Ravine, then we'll head out."

Benton understood and nodded. He sang out names

and men reined forward. He led them in a tight lope, angling southerly. Foster Gorman watched them go for a while then spoke aside to a big rawboned older man beside him. The older man merely grunted at him; he was one of the ranchers whose cattle had been rustled; he did not want to talk, he wanted to shoot.

" Hey," he called forward to Clint, his voice mean-sounding. " Their horses are worse off than ours. Let's make a rush and get this over with."

Clint, watching Benton's party get smaller, said nothing. Behind him the Texans murmured; there was a hard whisper made by guns being drawn over leather. Welker reined up and stopped. He studied the sheriff's profile a moment before speaking.

" Funny thing about people," he grunted finally. " Don't matter whether they're Mexes or females— they got to keep pushin' a man, don't they?"

Clint's head came slowly around. He fixed the cow-boy with a long impassive stare and inclined his head a little without speaking. Johnny was encouraged.

" They got to keep pushing. Got to keep trying their luck. You'd think Mex rustlers'd learn after while it don't pay—raidin' up into Texas. But they never do."

" No."

" And women . . . Just can't leave a man alone. Got to make him over. Got to . . ."

" Let's go !" Clint called backwards and rowelled his mount. Benton's men were no longer in sight. He did not look at Johnny Welker.

They broke over, at first, into a heavy gallop. A mile farther on they picked up speed. Hoofbeats drummed against hard ground and the swish of horses's legs through the buffalo grass made a whipping sound. Clint unshipped his carbine; held it one-handed across his lap. On either side of him rode Welker and Foster Gorman, both young, both eager.

Distantly, came the flung-back flat echo of a gunshot. Every man riding with Clint tensed a little; raised their naked weapons and dug harder with the spurs. They were racing swiftly over the plain now, their one thought to get as close as possible before the rustlers broke out of Chavez Ravine.

" Yonder they go," a man called sharply.

The Mexicans were swarming up out of the Ravine, a few erupting over the northern barranca but most of them charging away to the south.

Foster Gorman tried a long carbine shot. It hit no one but it spurred the Mexicans to desperate efforts. They did not seek escape in a body, but instead broke away riding separately or in pairs, quirts rising and falling, horses straining in a belly-down run. Clint's Texans let off a wild yell and swerved away after individual rustlers. Gunshots increased and before the men were close to one another there was, first a little grey burst of smoke, then seconds later, the report.

Foster Gorman stayed with the sheriff. It was a wild ride. The Mexicans were good riders, but, like the Texans, they shot often without hitting anything. The plunging back of a racing horse was not conducive to marksmanship.

South of the Ravine Benton's crew showed briefly, then was lost in swirling dust as the men spurred grimly after the main body of rustlers. Clint could hear their diminishing gunfire turn soft in the distance.

It was like an Indian fight; there was no order, no organisation, no quarter. Each man selected a target and stayed after it until he either ran his horse down, exhausted his ammunition, or killed his prey. Clint Verrill did not take part in the mêlée, instead he rode cautiously to the Ravine's rim, dismounted, crept forward, lay flat and poked his head over watching for movement.

There were cattle down there, made nervous by the sudden excitement but too foot-sore to stampede and too bewildered and unfamiliar with the arroyo they were in to know where to run. They bawled and moved uneasily here and there making it difficult for Clint to determine if there were any rustlers down there among them. Not until Welker rode up on his winded mount, got down and crept forward to lie beside Clint did the sheriff locate what he was seeking.

" Four saddled horses," he said abruptly. " Dragging their reins, Johnny. See them?"

" No."

" Follow out the creek there. Near that big old black-oak part way across the bottoms."

" I see them," Welker said, his voice turning sharp and exultant. " Let's go down."

Clint threw out a hand. " Relax," he ordered. " They aren't going anywhere. Wait until the others come up."

" They might make a run for it."

The sheriff patted his carbine significantly. " They'll

have to be pretty desperate to try it," he said. "We could pick them off from up here like shooting fish in a rain-barrel."

They continued to lie there, the violent summer sun blasting them, until other possemen jogged up and got down, some waving aloft Mexican gun-belts or weapons and a few leading captured horses with great-pommelled Mex saddles on them, then Clint left Welker to continue the vigil while he went back to the others.

Carl Benton's crew had not yet returned and three of his own men still gone but he still had five men. Before he could say anything though, dark, stolid Bruce Gollar shook his head heavily and growled loud enough for them all to hear.

"We got a nasty job to do, boys."

"What?" Someone demanded shortly.

"Foster's out there . . ."

Clint stared at the dark cowboy. "Foster . . .?"

"Right through the heart."

No one spoke. Clint looked down. Young Foster Gorman . . . It was hard to believe. He'd only been married a few weeks. That was what Gollar had meant : someone would have to tell his young bride that Foster would not be coming back.

A lean, stooped man swore with soft bitterness. Someone else, looking southward, saw Johnny Welker lying still and said : "Johnny too?"

Clint roused himself. "No : he's watching. There are three or four of them that didn't make it. They're still down there."

B

Bruce Gollar lifted his carbine and moved off. The others followed him. Johnny came back beating dust off his clothing. He told Clint he thought the rustlers were hiding in the willows but wasn't certain.

" The thing is," he concluded. " How do we get down there without gettin' shot? There's no cover at all until a man's plumb down in there."

Clint shrugged. He had already noticed the lack of cover and had decided there was nothing to do but just start down one of the trails and, if fired upon, to run crouched and zig-zag; there was nothing else a man could do. " Leave the horses," he said, moving forward toward the same trail the stolen cattle had been driven down. " Bob; you and Cal stay with them."

The men loomed upon the northern barranca, angled along it on foot as far as the trail and plunged over for the descent. Every man had his gun at the ready.

Clint had surmised correctly that the hiding Mexicans would not open fire; would not in fact do anything which might attract attention to them, hoping the Texans would simply round up their recovered cattle and ride away. It was, Clint thought, what he would have done under reversed circumstances.

He got down into the ravine easily and led the possemen into some shadowed covert. It was blessedly cool down there. Feed, brush and trees grew profusely. Clearly, the sun struck only briefly into this huge depression and it was therefore never as dehydrated as the overhead plain.

" They'll probably be together," Clint told his companions. " Johnny; take a couple of boys and see if you can get those saddled horses we saw."

" All right."

" Wait a minute," a man called sharply, stopping Welker in his tracks. " I saw movement over along the creek."

" Cattle," someone murmured.

"Not by a darn sight," the cowboy exclaimed strongly. " Man-movement; close to the ground and sort of gliding."

Clint dropped to one knee straining to see ahead where the willow-bank twisted and turned over the ravine's floor. No one spoke; hot silence settled.

" Well," an impatient Texan said. " whatever you seen ain't moving now."

There was the nearly inaudible sound of a gun butt brushing cloth. Clint swung around. " Hold it," he commanded, and the cowboy training his weapon upon the willows looked down at him.

" What the hell for?" He growled.

Clint did not answer. He faced forward and called out : " *Ojé! Paisanos! Fuera! Undale pronto! Venga!*"

There was no reply. The Texans dropped low, waiting, every face resolutely set and uncompromising. " You're wastin' time," a man said harshly. " They aren't going to come out."

The same cowboy Clint had stopped from firing prematurely now moved forward into plain sight and threw up his gun. He never got a chance to fire; a crashing fusillade broke the stillness and the Texan went over backwards as though struck hard by an invisible sledge. He fell into a flourishing big sage bush and hung there, dead.

With cries of fury Clint's remaining men poured a volley into the far willows where gunsmoke drifted lazily then sprang up and raced forward. There was no reasoning, no caution or logic in their charge; they were simply enraged frontiersmen beyond caring. They fired from the hip as they ran. Willows, cut through by bullets, fell, and those not cut whipped and bent under the storm of lead.

A lean, young Mexican sprang out to face his enemies. He was handsomely garbed in a leather Charro suit with embroidery of silver and gold thread worked into intricate designs.

Clint could plainly see white teeth beyond the carbine, wild dark eyes flashing, then he ducked when the Mexican fired, dropped his own carbine, swept up his six-gun and fired twice from a range of less than three hundred feet. The Mexican went down. As he arose, or attempted to, a flurry of shots flattened him.

Captive echoes filled the arroyo, deafening in themselves even without the gunfire. From somewhere overhead there arose a hoarse cry followed immediately by the reckless plunge of Carl Benton's men downward into the bottoms. The firing increased. Clint retrieved his carbine and sprang for cover as two Mexicans began calling for quarter. One of them made a fatal mistake; he walked out into plain sight with his carbine held overhead in both hands, a token of surrender. He was cut down in a twinkling.

From farther back in the willows the lone surviving rustler kept up a steady cry for quarter. Clint added his own voice to the din ordering his possemen to hold their fire. He was successful only when the Texans could find nothing to shoot at and stopped firing of their own volition. He went in search of Johnny, found him talking to Carl Benton, and told them both to see that no one fired while he went in after the rustler. They agreed but with considerable reluctance.

The Mexican had been shot and while the wound was not serious—one ear had been torn away—he was covered with blood and was convinced he was dying. He beseeched Clint to halt the bleeding and called upon his patron saint for succour.

Clint tore the back out of the man's shirt, bound his wound and disarmed him. The Mexican was ashen and trembling. He constantly implored Clint to save him from being lynched. Clint made no promises and led him out where the Texans were waiting. One look at that beetling, savage crew and the Mexican fell to his knees praying and writhing. Johnny Welker reflected the attitude of his companions. He watched the terrified rustler a moment, then said a contemptuous bitter word, holstered his six-gun and began rolling a cigarette.

The sun was a red ball low upon the horizon before all the cattle were gotten onto the plain overhead and strung out towards Travis. Bumping along softly in the rear of the drive were several bodies, among them the cowboy who had been killed in the ravine, and young Foster Gorman.

Except for Clint's insistence the Texans would have left the rustlers where they had fallen to be devoured by coyotes and buzzards; even after acceding to his orders though, they had lashed the Mexicans across their saddles indifferently and led them along with disgruntled, grim faces.

Travis was in sight against the reddening sky of evening when the cowmen split off with their riders, pushing the cattle towards the ranges from which they had been stolen; only Bruce Gollar and Johnny Welker headed for town with the sheriff, each of them leading at least one tired horse with its grisly burden.

" Clint?"

" Yeah."

" You want me to tell her?"

The sheriff shook his head. " Thanks, Johnny, but I think it's my place to do that."

" I don't envy you one damned bit."

Gollar echoed this and added : " Folks'll want to string up our gory-lookin' friend here." He glowered at the injured Mexican. " I'd sort of like to have a hand in that myself."

Clint made a cigarette. He said nothing until he had it lighted. " You know better than that, Bruce," was all he said, and Gollar, without looking convinced, nevertheless held his peace.

They did not get back to town until after nightfall and because Clint suspected some of the cowboys had ridden in first, anxious to tell of the fight, he approached the town from the west, avoided its main roadway, and got to the horse-shed behind his office-jail combination unobserved; he knew perfectly well the reaction Foster Gorman's killing would have on the populace : It wasn't that he felt duty-bound to protect his prisoner from being taken out and lynched, it was simply that he had never lost a prisoner to a mob and did not mean to lose this one either. Like all frontier Texans Clint Verrill rationalised about the law; he did not hold with mob-justice but on the other hand he believed in swift and merciless punishment for the guilty. He believed this simply because, in a land of outlaws and killers, only the fear of retribution and the fast guns of those who were legally endowed with the right of enforcing justice, kept more men from turning to lawlessness.

Simply, the philosophy of Sheriff Verrill was as he had tried often to explain it to Florence Berry : Might was right and might was in the holsters of the law. Until enforceable justice made South Texas safe for law-abiding people there had to be men willing and able to discourage, even kill if necessary, those who would hold back progress.

He thought of that after he had locked the prisoner in a cell and was making coffee for the three of them. He knew everyone in Travis, including Florence would know by morning what had happened at Chavez Ravine. He knew too that the majority of them would demand he deliver the prisoner up to a kangaroo court.

He was tired. Not only from the chase and the fight, but also from the knowledge of what still lay ahead; the bitterness, the recrimination, the bracing into wrath. Johnny Welker roused him, turned his thoughts away from unpleasantness with a question.

"You going to see Grace Gorman tonight?"

"Yes. Otherwise she'll hear it from someone else, Johnny."

"Yeah."

Welker went glumly to the stove and re-filled his cup with coffee. From that part of the room he said: "Did Foster have any kin hereabouts?"

Clint shrugged. He did not know. In fact, actually, he knew very little about Foster Gorman. He had drifted into Travis two years previously as a round-up rider, one of that restless, drifting breed of itinerant cowboys that came and went. He had settled down and married. That was everything Clint knew about him—that—and the fact that Foster had been a good hand, well-liked, not troublesome, and young. It was a definition which fit hundreds of range-riders. No one asked personal questions; it not only wasn't polite to do so, it wasn't healthy either. What lay in a man's past was his private concern and was no one else's business. Like all Texans, Clint Verrill observed this rule scrupulously unless a stranger got troublesome.

"Well," Johnny summed it up. "They come and they go. I reckon, except for little Grace, Foster'd be just another one of us that put his life on the line and lost."

"Except for Grace," the sheriff murmured, "that'd be about the size of it."

Chapter Two

CLINT LEFT WELKER and Gollar guarding the prisoner and went, not to Grace Gorman's home, but to Florence Berry's hotel room. There, under the solemn gaze of dark blue eyes he recounted what had happened at Chavez Ravine and when he was finished he asked Florence to accompany him to the Gorman place. He had anticipated that Foster Gorman's youthful widow would need a woman on hand when he told her Foster was dead, and he was correct. Grace Gorman went to pieces.

He left Florence with her and went up-town. There were times when a man needed a drink badly and this was one of them. But everything in life having its price, in order to get that drink he had to submit to a questioning by the men who were already at the saloon and who heard about the brush with the rustlers. For Clint it was an ordeal, not because of the questions particularly but because of what came next.

"Listen boys," a grizzled rangeman cried over the buzz of talk. "Listen a minute. This happens too often. Chasin' them, killing a few, doesn't stop them. I figure it this way," the cowman looked at his audience. " We got to make a real good example of one of these fellers."

Clint, leaning on the bar with his back to the room, could feel the depth of the ensuing silence; could feel the rapport existing between the cowman and his listeners and knew what it meant. He finished his drink, saw the barman's steady gaze on him, and turned.

" We'll make a good example of him," he said quietly, in a tone none of the men in that crowded room misinterpreted. " When the circuit judge gets here."

The cowman's long stare hardened. " We're not blaming you," he told Clint. " We're blaming the raiders and we got to teach them a lesson they'll never forget."

" Oh?" Clint asked. " How?"

" Make us up a posse and ride down over the line and catch us a few of them devils and hang 'em in their own doorways, that's how."

There was a murmur of assent. Even the barman, whose vocation usually demanded strict neutrality, inclined his head in agreement.

The whisky warmed Clint; it tingled out along his nerves and worked at alleviating the weariness. He drew up a little against the bar. " You're talking like a fool," he told the cowman. " You'd likely start a war with Mexico."

" Who cares?" Someone cried angrily from the back of the room. " We licked them once and we can lick 'em again."

"Maybe," Clint replied, keeping his voice calm with an effort. "But I doubt it. You wouldn't just be fighting Mexicans, you'd have U.S. troops on your necks too."

"Aw," the cowman scoffed. "They'd help us—not fight us."

"You're not showing much sense," retorted Clint, his voice sounding thin-edged now. "Soldiers obey orders. If Texans invaded Mexico our government'd send its troops after the Texans. If they didn't kill you, boys, the Mexicans would. But if neither side did and you got out of it with a whole skin you'd be fugitives for life—and you'd probably be caught someday and hung." He flagged for another drink and the barman obeyed quickly. Clint downed it watching the crowd, then he set the glass down and fixed the grizzled cowman with an unfriendly stare.

"I think you've had your say now. I reckon you'd better ride on."

The cowman flushed dark red. He shifted his feet and groped for the initiative he'd lost. "What about that boy that was killed?" He demanded harshly. "What about his little widow?"

Remembering what Johnny Welker had said, Clint repeated it now. "He laid his life on the line and he lost. We've all taken the same risk some time or other. If every time one of us got the deep six the rest of us went raiding down into Mexico we wouldn't be any better that the raiders who come up here and you know it." He drew back a big breath. "I'm as sorry about Foster as any of you—sorrier probably because

I knew him better. But I'm not going to start a war over him and neither are you. Now mister, you get on your horse and ride on out of town until you cool off."

The cowman left. A number of riders went with him. Most of the saloon's patrons returned to their previous occupations of gambling or drinking or just visiting. The barman leaned across from Clint with a thoughtful and frowning face.

" It hasn't ended," he said. " Folks've had just about enough of them greasers raidin' up here."

Clint did not reply. As far as he was concerned the conversation was closed. " You got any fresh onions?" He asked.

" Yeah; a fresh bunch from Sonora. Got some fresh lemons too."

" Give me a bowl of the onions and a cold glass of beer."

When the bowl appeared Clint took it, and the stein of beer, to a wall table and sank down there. He ran his legs out their full length and relaxed. Maybe the bartender was right; maybe the people of Travis and the cowmen of the back-country had had enough, he thought. They certainly had reason enough to go on the warpath even without Foster Gorman's killing to incite them. Mexican raiders had been coming over the line since long before he'd come into office as sheriff. And it was time something was done about it, too. He would not argue against that. But it was up to the Federal Government to initiate action not the people of Travis. Maybe even the Texas government at Austin was responsible for stopping the raiders. He sipped beer and grimaced. No; the state government consisted of men like that grizzled cowman; if it went into action it would do so in the same fashion.

" Hello Clint."

He looked up. It was Will Custer. Will not only owned and operated Travis's only newspaper—*The Lone Star Review*—he was a member of the Town Council.

" Hello Will."

" Mind if I sit down?"

" No. You want a drink?"

Custer sat. He wagged his head negatively. " I'd like to print the facts about what happened out at Chavez Ravine."

Clint told him what had happened in as few words as possible, finished the bowl of onions, drained off the beer and worked up a cigarette. Will Custer held a match for him.

" Folks are pretty stirred up," he told the sheriff.

" They're always stirred up after a raid."

" It's not the raid, Clint. It's Foster Gorman they're stirred up about this time."

Clint exhaled. " He's not the first killing we've had in one of those scrapes, Will."

" No; but you know the people. Clint. When they've had enough they don't rationalise—they act."

Clint smoked thoughtfully for a moment, then he said : " Will; on the off-chance that you're right I think the Town Council ought to write the government at Austin."

" What for?"

" Request troops be stationed here for a while. Until the excitement simmers down."

Will Custer's nostrils flared. " That'd only make things worse," he said, and it was clear that he would be one of those to whom the garrisoning of Travis by U.S. troops—the victors over their own Confederacy not too many years earlier—would be anathema.

Clint understood and sighed. " All right; do whatever you like," he told the newspaperman, " but Will —I'm going to tell you one thing. No one takes that prisoner away from me." He paused and gazed out over the noisy room. " And I'll tell you something else too. The first man who rides out of Travis heading for Mexico with blood in his eye is going to wind up in my jail."

Will Custer drummed on the table a moment, then flagged for a drink. As the barman approached he said : " Want a refill, Clint?"

" No thanks."

The sheriff got up, nodded and started for the door. Behind him Will Custer's gaze followed his progress.

Beyond the saloon's noise and smoke Travis lay darkened and somnolent. There were two guttering coach lamps on either side of the doorless opening at Houston's livery barn and beneath them some idlers stood in the warm night talking. Farther along the plank-walk and also across the roadway orange lamp-light showed through the grilled windows of the sheriff's office. Clint was in no hurry to return there.

He strolled south with the strong sound of his booted

feet striking hard against the walkway-planking, breathing deeply of the fresh darkness and carefully thinking of what Will Custer had said. It would all die down he told himself. It always had. The fact that Foster Gorman had been killed aggravated things, yes, but there had been other killings under identical circumstances and while tempers ran short then too, time had assuaged them.

It was not simply a matter of convincing himself this was true that made his tenseness depart, it was the additional knowledge that both townsmen and cowmen knew what would surely follow any rash act on their part.

He made a cigarette in the gloom before O'Farrell's general store; leaned upon an overhang upright smoking it and recalling those unnerving moments with Grace Gorman. Women were something he did not really know much about. He had never been married and had only indifferently courted girls, but in the soft night he remembered the strange, long look Florence had given him before he'd left the Gorman place. It was not a look an inexperienced man could define nor decipher.

He was still thinking of that look when a woman's short, lighter steps came upward toward him along the plank-walk. He did not have to look to know whose footfalls they were.

She saw him and slowed. He turned easily, hat back and wide shoulders relaxed into a long slope.

"Thanks, Florence. I don't think I'd have been much good down there without you."

She stopped, pale oval face solemn in the dimness. She seemed unable to find the words she sought. " I—Clint; what will become of her now?"

" Well," he answered slowly, " she has folks. She'll go back to them I reckon."

" I didn't mean that. I meant—what is her future? How will the wrenching away of a love like that affect her?"

He wanted to say Grace Gorman wasn't the only gunshot-widow in the West. Instead he shrugged gently and said nothing.

" You can't be that callous," Florence exclaimed sharply, looking closely into his face in the gloom. " Texas doesn't make everyone like that, does it?"

" Texas," he replied quietly, " is a long way from Boston, Florence. It's not like Massachusetts at all."

" It certainly isn't !"

" But someday it will be."

" I doubt that very much."

He went on as though he had not heard. " Until it is, as I've told you before, there will be violence."

" But—every week; every few days?"

" Yes; every few days. Listen Florence; Massachusetts was like that a hundred years ago." He drew up against the post at his back. " I reckon Massachusetts men acted about like Texans act now, and I expect their womenfolk didn't always want 'em to turn the other cheek or run away."

" Clint; you could have sent for the soldiers. That was their job—catching those raiders."

He tossed down the cigarette and regarded its guttering small red tip in the roadway dust. " Fort Lincoln is thirty-two miles north of Travis. If we'd waited for troops from up there we'd have lost not just the raiders but the cattle as well."

" But Foster would be alive, Clint."

His jaw muscles rippled and he did not raise his eyes. In fact an interval of silence passed before he spoke again, then all he said was : " I reckon. Good night, Florence. And thanks again. I appreciate that; other folks will too, believe me."

" Clint!"

He checked himself and turned back. They exchanged a long glance. Her stare went deep into him, knife-like. He waited.

" I will be going back next week . . ."

He considered this. She had come to Travis to dispose of some property she had inherited from a distant relative. She had been there nearly a month now. He did not, in his present weary state of mind, comprehend right away.

" So soon?" he said.

" Yes. I've accomplished what I came here for."

" I see."

" Clint? Go back with me."

He drew in a silent big breath and exhaled it. They had discussed this before. " Wish I could," he answered. " For a visit anyway. But I can't."

" Why? Why can't you?"

He smiled at her. " Well; for one thing when folks vote a man in as sheriff they expect him to be on the job, not gallivantin' all over the country."

C

" Is that all?"

" No."

She waited for him to enlarge and when he did not she said : " What else?"

" Just a feeling I've got. I couldn't put it into words, Florence."

She continued there in the gloom without speaking, studying his face a while longer, then she nodded and started on toward the hotel. He watched her, wanting to call her name, to catch up and prolong their conversation, but he did neither and when she turned in farther along the walkway he started for the sheriff's office.

Johnny Welker let him in. Bruce Gollar was sprawled in slumber on a pallet in an open cell. Johnny yawned and ran a hand over his cheek making a scratchy sound. " Couple fellers came around a while back to see you," he told Clint.

" Who were they?"

" One was Carl Benton. I didn't know the other one. Looked like a cowman though."

" Carl say anything?"

" Yeah. He said the Town Council had discussed holding a private hearing for your prisoner."

Clint stopped in mid-stride toward the coffee pot on the stove, turned and scowled. " They can't do that, dammit. They got no authority for anything like that."

" Don't tell me," Welker shot back, " tell them."

Clint continued on to the stove, poured a cup of coffee and looked inquiringly at Welker. The cowboy shook his head. " I've drunk so much of that stuff tonight I figure to turn black by morning." He watched Clint sip, and his expression was critical. "You work for the Town Council," he ventured. "If they give you orders you have to obey them don't you?"

"Not when I'm ordered to do something illegal, Johnny, like turning the Mexican over to a lynch-crowd."

"They got the power to replace you, Clint. They could appoint some feller who'd go along with them."

Sheriff Verrill shook his head. "Carl's not likely to go along with anything like that. I don't think Will Custer would either." He hung the tin cup back on its nail behind the stove. "Anyway; I'm not giving up this prisoner to anyone." He went to a chair and sank down, tossed his hat on the desk and narrowed his eyes. After what Custer had said in the saloon he was not so sure but that Will would make some effort to expedite the prisoner's trial, one way or another.

"Well; if you don't need me any more tonight, Clint . . ."

"No. And thanks, Johnny."

"S'long Sheriff."

"Adios."

It was nearly two o'clock in the morning. Travis was totally quiet. Clint went once to the door, looked both ways along the roadway, then locked himself in and retired to the unoccupied pallet across the cell from Bruce Gollar. He did not dream this night; he was not even aware that day had come until someone banged with a pistol butt on the roadside door.

It was two of the local cowboys who had been with

the posse at Chavez Ravine, Bob Stewart and Cal Lounsberry. Both wanted to know if they'd get into trouble with the law for selling the horses they had brought back with them and which had formerly belonged to the rustlers. Clint told them they would not as long as they gave proper bills-of-sale. Lounsberry and Stewart left broadly smiling. Clint watched them head straight for Caleb Houston's livery barn.

He cleaned himself up, made some coffee and whacked the bottom of Bruce Gollar's boots to awaken the dark man. Gollar came out of it dazedly, sniffed the coffee and went out front to the water trough and scrubbed.

They drank coffee together then Gollar left. He was regularly employed by a cow outfit over near the Quanah Buttes country.

The day passed quietly enough. Clint stayed close but neither Custer nor Benton appeared. He interrogated his prisoner, whose name was Francisco Amador, caught up on his rest, made his rounds, and that night visited the saloons. There, he ran across Benton. The blacksmith was a little dour about the prisoner but agreed that he had the right of a fair trial.

For four days Travis continued relatively placid. The antagonism aroused by the latest rustler-raid did not die, but it seemed to diminish. At least Will Custer's newspaper which was the weathervane of opinion and sentiment around Travis, came finally to editorialising less and less about raiders from south of the border.

For Sheriff Verrill this was a time of comparative inactivity and he enjoyed it. Twice he wired ahead to ascertain when the circuit judge would appear at Travis to hold court. The judge had been detained by an involved trial sixty miles east; both his answers were indefinite.

The last night of Florence Berry's stay in Travis Clint took her for a buggyride. There was a lopsided old moon to light the way and a scattering of pearl-like stars shimmering like cast-down diamonds. The night was warm and alive for them, the land strongly, pungently fragrant with the biting aroma of South Texas plains. He drove effortlessly letting the buggy-horse amble along on a loose line. A man felt sad at a time like this; parting was more than sorrow for the Texan. His life was at best unsure and the substance of memories was precious. He could only hope to preserve the one; the other, memories, he knew must inevitably fade, must be ravaged by time, must perish finally with time's passage. Out of these reflections he could only conclude that life was, as he'd felt all along, a transitory experience, a period of struggle and hardship—and now, this last night, of pain as well.

He roused himself with effort groping for something light to say. The words failed him. He made a cigarette and lit it. Pale smoke eddied into the windless night. There was a solid core of incoherence in him. He felt many things instinctively, intuitively, but he was a common man and feeling something, knowing it, was different from expressing it.

"You are quiet tonight," Florence said finally, encouraging him to speak.

"There are a lot of things a man wonders about," he told her musingly.

"Not only men, Clint. Women wonder too."

"Well; what drove you to Texas, Florence, and what made me see in you something I've never seen in any other girl before?"

She considered this in long silence, watching the shadows loom up gently and drift away rearward as the buggy passed, and when she might have replied he broke in to pursue his thoughts.

"We belong to different worlds. You should've stayed in Boston. You'd have met some man there . . . I should've found a Texas girl . . ." He killed the cigarette against the whip-socket and tossed it out. "A man wonders about things like that. Life's hard enough as it is—why do things like this have to happen?"

She looked at him with a gentle smile. "I'm flattered," she said. "What you're saying is that you're fond of me, Clint."

He looked around in an expressionless way. "That's no secret. Even over at Chavez Ravine there was some talk about that." He looped the lines and thumbed back his hat. "We're not kids, Florence. I'm in love with you. I don't have to get all panicky when I tell you that. Anyway, you know it's true. The trouble is —where it ought to simplify things—it doesn't. It makes them harder."

She brushed his arm with her fingers. "Please Clint; come with me. You don't belong in a savage country like this. You belong in the East. You're a smart man; you'd make your mark there in business or in politics or—"

" Why does it always end this way?" he interrupted to demand of her. " I'm a Texan. I belong in Texas. My people started the work of making this a civilised country. They whipped the Comanches, the Mexicans; they left a lot undone and my generation's job is to finish it."

She murmured : " You feel that very strongly, don't you?"

Instead of answering he took up the lines and headed toward a little knoll where pine trees stood starkly against the night, stopped there and got down. She too alighted when he went to her side and held up his hand. As they stood thus, face to face and quite close, she said : " Clint; that's what sets Texans apart, isn't it? This feeling they have about shaping destiny; about finishing the work their parents started. I've encountered it many times since coming here. Texans are a kind of people; a special kind."

Again without speaking he led her to the dripping darkness of the pines and sank down. She went down beside him breathing deeply of the night-clean air.

" I believe in what my folks worked towards," he said eventually, looking straight away over the prairie and speaking as though to himself. " I wish I could convince you how things will be here someday, Florence. I wish you'd see that the place of a loved woman is beside the man who loves her."

She was regarding her hands in her lap and he could

not see the mistiness of her eyes nor their deepening colour. He only heard her reply and it was very soft. " A woman wants what is best in life for her lover, Clint. If she knows he is capable of great things she will not settle for less, for him." Her head came up. " Not this, Clint. Not this riding out with guns. Not this dust and turmoil and everlasting uncertainty."

After a moment he said, either wearily or resignedly : " I don't think we're even talking about the same things, Florence. I want to make Texas into what your East is, and you don't understand that someone has to pioneer any land to make it law-abiding and civilised."

" I understand," she quickly replied. " I just don't see why it must be you who is the pioneer."

" And if everyone in Texas felt that way—what then?"

" But everyone doesn't, Clint."

" No, Florence, they don't. And I'm one of them."

He arose and held out his hand. She came up off the ground gracefully. There was a hardness to his face, an uncompromising flintiness, and when he spoke again some of the bitterness was in his words.

" If worlds separate us," he said, speaking harshly, " at least we can meet on one common ground." He reached forward touching her with both hands. She saw the moving black cut of his shoulders against the night; the lowering blur of his face and he was not smiling. For a second he hung there, his mouth close to her lips. " Something to remember," he said. " Something of you I'll keep here in Texas forever; something of me you will take back to Boston."

The pressure on her upper arms grew greater drawing her to him. She lifted her face, brought up both hands to place them palms forward against his chest without pressure. She met his lips squarely, as a woman not as a girl. She felt the heaviness of his mouth with its longing and its hunger. Also, she had in that moment an awakening of realisation about Clint Verrill all the words in the world had not and could not, make clear to her. His kiss let loose the force of his will, the unbending iron of his temper, the force and pressure of a man whose convictions were unalterable. When he stepped back she had to call up reserves of strength to maintain an unfaltering equilibrium and even then she swayed slightly, not entirely from the kiss, but also from the revelation.

He was studying her face. Instinct told her to keep from him what she had discovered; she made a small smile looking squarely into his eyes.

" Thank you, Clint," she said, " for giving me something to take back with me."

He led her to the buggy and handed her up, went around to the driver's side and climbed in beside her. The old mare turned without guidance and began slow-pacing the night back towards Travis.

" A kiss," he told her, after a while and speaking with some bitterness, " is always, in every book I've ever read, sort of a prelude to happiness." He bent a long look around at her. " A person never gets too old to learn, do they? That kiss was an end of something, Florence—an end of happiness."

She did not reply until Travis lay dead ahead low

and ugly and light splashed. " It wasn't final," she said, then. His head came around swiftly, the eyes wide in query. " Clint; I love you. I suppose I could even come to love Texas. But life is not long—I want you to prove yourself. I want to see you forge ahead." She looked from his face to the functional black square-ness of the town ahead. " Not here, where the best we could hope for is so awfully limited—but where—"

" Where people are civilised," he said sharply, almost angrily, and locked his jaws hard for a moment making muscle-shadows ripple. " Florence; I would rather make civilisation any day in this damned world, then live in it after someone else has done the real work—like the people you call civilised do !"

They did not speak again until he had escorted her to the hotel entrance. There, with pain to witness it, he removed his hat while gazing solemnly down into her eyes, and said : " Good-bye, Florence."

She steadied herself upon the doorjamb watching him stride with unnatural stiffness southward toward his office. She did not turn away until the night en-gulfed him; until the distant closing of a heavy oaken door broke her spell with strong finality.

Along Travis's single wide roadway horsemen jogged past, their drawling Texas voices musical in the still-ness. Somewhere beyond town a dog barked, and closer, from the doorless maw of Houston's livery barn, came the diluted imprecations of someone angered by the stubbornness of a horse.

Carl Benton and Will Custer, sitting on a bench in front of the *Drovers' & Merchants' Bank* of South Texas, watched the sheriff's leave-taking of Florence Berry in grave silence, then exchanged a long look, still without speaking. Moments later when neither Clint nor Florence were in view, Custer philosophised that such an affair could have had no other ending. The blacksmith though, after a quiet moment of reflection, held a contrary view.

" One thing I learnt a long time ago about folks in love," he said, " is that it's a lot easier for them to fight than it is for them to get along—at the start. Now those two—they both think it's all over between them. Well; like I said; it's easier for them to believe that than it is for either of 'em to believe love doesn't end that simply. Nope, Will; I'll give you five-to-one odds they get together."

Custer squinted down the road toward the sheriff's office where lamplight shone. " All right," he said agreeably. " I'll take that bet, Carl. Five-to-one." He expectorated into the roadway dust. " She's paid for a seat out o' town on the morning stage. If she takes it you owe me five dollars."

But the blacksmith was not willing to agree that the simple departure of Florence Berry from Travis was the end of it and said so. " The only time I'll pay you," he said, " is when he gets married to someone else, or she never comes back to him."

Custer scowled. " Hell," he exclaimed. " He might not marry for ten years."

Benton wagged his head. " You don't want to bet on that, too, do you? He'll marry, and it won't take any ten years for him to do it either."

They might have pursued the argument further but a band of riders struck the roadway from the north and whirled past in a rattle of hoofs and exuberant cat-calls, heading for a saloon.

" Come on," Benton said, arising, " I'll buy you a drink."

They went forward toward the settling dust-cloud churned up by the rangemen and did not see Sheriff Verrill emerge from his office to stand quietly at the hitchrail looking northward where the boisterous riders had stopped. Neither did they see the lean, jaunty figure that came up behind Clint to pause, looking past in the same direction the lawman was gazing.

" Going to be one of those nights," the slouching figure said. " They're from Jack Morton's ranch."

Clint turned, recognising the voice. " Maybe I'll need a deputy, Johnny."

But Welker dissented. " Naw. They're just out to howl a little. JM doesn't have a mean rider on the pay-roll." He swung his attention to Clint's face, cocked his head a little and said : " You look like someone stole your best horse."

Clint made a mirthless small grin. " Maybe they did. How come you're in town tonight?"

" Getting low on money and getting tired of loafing. Figured I'd see what cowmen came in tonight and hit one or two of 'em up for a job."

Clint nodded understandingly and moved as though to enter the office. Welker, watching him closely, waited to speak until Clint was framed in the doorway.

" She's leavin' on the morning stage. That's it isn't it, Clint?"

" That's it, Johnny."

" Yeah," Welker said softly. " Well; if you want to drown your sorrow I'll be over at the *Parker House Saloon.*" He made a wry face. " 'Course, if it's a real big sorrow, why I won't have enough money to drown all of it." He smiled and started forward along the plank-walk.

Clint did not go to the Parker House or any other saloon until it was time to make his final rounds for the night and by that time neither Johnny Welker nor the JM riders were still around.

He retired early and arose the same way. After feeding Francisco Amador he forked hay to his horse in the shed behind the sheriff's office, then went to Bert Franklin's shop, had a haircut and shave, and ate a late breakfast for which he felt no need whatsoever.

At ten o'clock the north-bound stage was hooked up. At ten minutes after ten the passengers came out to board it and Clint went forward to help Florence with her bags. It was a bitter and awkward moment for them both. For a moment, before he handed her up into the coach, they stood close. She read without effort his undisguised pain and he, in turn, saw the dry-burning light in her eyes. He wanted to kiss her; to at least touch her hair, her face. Instead he brushed her fingers fleetingly as they moved towards the coach through the press of other people, held the door for her and after she was seated he turned deliberately away to throw her luggage up to the driver where it was strapped along with other bags atop the battered old Concord. A moment later, with a shout, a rattle of chain-harness, the grinding of steel tyres into the eternal Texas dust, the stage drew away.

He stood to the last with people eddying around him, conscious of his agony and fighting against letting it show; then a familiar voice said : " Come on; you need a drink." It was Johnny Welker again.

The alcohol though, failed in its purpose. Johnny could see this from his position beside the sheriff and suggested a game of cards. They played, but again the sheriff was indifferent. He was miles away somehow and did not play well. But Johnny persisted and it was a valiant effort too. He kept at it until early afternoon thinking as a man might who had, himself, never been infected by a sentiment lasting more than an hour or two, that six or seven hours would suffice to either ameliorate the pain or at least dull it.

It was impossible to guess how long Welker would have persevered because at four o'clock a sweat- and dust-covered cowboy thundered into town yelling for the sheriff. Clint was roused by the excitement and ran out into the roadway with everyone else, Johnny Welker at his side.

" It's the coach, Sheriff. It's lying on its side about ten miles north o' here," the rider gasped, holding out a crumpled paper. " Someone took the horses and the passengers . . . I come onto it accidental-like and found this here note stuck to one of the doors with a knife."

Johnny Welker edged close to where Clint was

studying the soiled piece of paper. He read, swore aloud, and read again.

"What's it say?" A man demanded from farther back, sounding annoyed.

Welker turned. "It says a bunch of raiders got the passengers and unless we turn Amador loose they'll kill them. That's what it says!"

Chapter Three

THE BOLDNESS of this fresh attack coming as it did before public sentiment was fully recovered from the killing of Foster Gorman, plus the fact that the raiders were openly defying the Texans by taking hostages, beat up a storm in Travis that grew greater as the day advanced and by nightfall the little cowtown was full of armed cowmen, their riders, irate townsmen, and even disinterested travellers who were demanding swift retaliation and volunteering to participate in it.

At the sheriff's office Carl Benton and Will Custer sat with Sheriff Verrill and Johnny Welker. Custer was fiercely angry at the sheriff.

"You fool," he cried. "You've *got* to let him go. Can't you get it through your thick skull that those rustlers'll kill their hostages?"

Clint's reply was coldly bitter. "Of course I know that," he told the newspaperman. "And I aim to release Amador. But not until I have posses along the southerly trails, Will, so I can capture those raiders after they've started back for Mexico."

"*No!*" Custer roared. "You can't take a chance like that. You've got to let them get away this time. Listen,

Clint," Custer's voice softened, turned almost pleading. "They'll have men out. You know that. If they see a bunch of us riding south they'll know we aim to cut them off from getting back over the line." Custer straightened up fixing the sheriff with his stare. "Think of Florence, Clint. Think what they'll do to her."

Welker interrupted. "Mr. Custer," he said acidly. "Seems like I recollect only a few days ago you breathin' fire and brimstone to make a few examples of those rustlers."

Custer whirled on the lithe younger man. "This is none of your business," he exclaimed. "Keep out of it."

"It's his business," the sheriff said stoutly. "Every time there's trouble he's deputised. He's put his life on the line two dozen times, Will, and for nothing. The least your stingy Town Council could do would be pay volunteer possemen for their time."

"That's beside the point, Clint. You can't do—"

"Wait a minute," Benton said, interrupting. "Just a second you two." When silence came Benton gazed out of squinted eyes at Clint. "You're not putting that girl's life on the line without a pretty good idea you're going to be able to save it. I know you better'n that. What's on your mind, Clint?"

"I want to make up four posses, Carl. I want someone to lead each one north, south, east, and west. Sure; I know the rustlers'll head south. But just in case they don't—just in case they're figuring to play this smart by going some way we wouldn't guess—I want crews out to stop them."

D

Will Custer would have broken in with another loud protest but Benton stopped him, then nodded at Clint. " Go on," he said quietly. " Let's have the rest of it."

" The posses'll ride out tonight—in the darkness, Carl. They'll be in position before sunup."

" That's a sound idea," Benton agreed. " The best trackers in the world are helpless in the dark. All right; I'll go along with that. I'll even lead one of the posses. Say, the one that heads south."

But Clint shook his head. " I'll lead that one," he said, and Johnny Welker's shrewd eyes narrowed in a humourless smile at the look on the sheriff's face.

Benton did not argue. Instead he faced the newspaperman. " What's wrong with that plan?" He challenged, and when Custer made no immediate reply Benton answered himself. " Nothing at all. Let's you'n me go organise the boys and bring everyone back here."

As Benton and Custer arose Clint stopped them. " Don't do anything for half an hour."

" Why not?"

" I'm going to release Amador and I don't want him to see everyone ready to ride out or he'll pass the word to his friends."

" Oh. All right."

After the councilmen had departed Johnny Welker chuckled and shook his head. " I thought for a while there Custer was going to fire you."

" He couldn't if he wanted to. It takes a unanimous vote of the Council for that."

" Want me to get the prisoner out here, Clint?"

"Not just yet, Johnny. The less he hears the better." Clint went to a wall-rack of guns and took down two carbines, checked their loads and tossed Welker one of the weapons. "You head up the west posse, Johnny. If I run into them to the south and they make a run for it like they did at Chavez Ravine, I'm guessing they'll head west so they can cross over farther along."

"All right. Benton'll head the north posse and Custer the east one. Right?"

Clint nodded "Good guess," he said.

But Welker demurred with a twinkle in his eyes. "About Custer it wasn't a guess. You'll want him as far away from you and as far from where he starts a war as possible. You don't figure those rustlers'll head east."

Clint smiled; the first time in two days. "Your badge is on the desk," he said, and Welker chuckled.

"Funny thing about you, Clint. When you don't want to answer a feller right out, you sort of slide around him by saying something to change the subject."

Clint got Francisco Amador from his cell. The Mexican was uneasy and not a little fearful so he smiled broadly. Johnny Welker's cold and expressionless regard did nothing to lessen the rustler's trepidation and he gazed inquiringly at the sheriff.

"*Señor*," he said. "*Señor jefe?*"

"Can you read English?" asked Clint offering the note.

"*No, Señor; no habla, escribe, no—*"

Clint read the note in Spanish and gazed at the outlaw. Slow comprehension dawned and Amador's wavering smile firmed up with understanding. He puffed out his cheeks and emitted a prodigious sigh. " I thought," he told Clint in Spanish, " I was going to perish from the rope. My fears were formidable."

" It may still happen," Welker said dryly.

The Mexican was bewildered. His smile faded; he looked from Welker's unmistakably unfriendly expression to Clint, and raised his eyebrows.

Clint did not interpret, instead he told Amador that he wanted him to remind his friends that the bargain was for them to release the hostages as soon as they had Amador back with them.

The Mexican was volubly reassuring; so reassuring in fact that Johnny turned his back in disgust and stood gazing out into the unnaturally empty roadway.

" *En aqui,*" Clint ordered, and accompanied Amador from the office. Walked with him steadily northward through a town so still, so empty of people, their footfalls echoed loudly in the quickening darkness of late evening. At the northernmost boundary of Travis Clint halted. " Keep walking," he told the rustler. " Your friends will find you. And Amador—remember; they are to release the *prisoneros.* It is understood?"

" *Oh, seguro, jefe. Si, si.*"

Clint watched the outlaw stride self-consciously away. He waited a full fifteen minutes before turning back, then hastened to the office. There, filling the roadway, was a night-blackened, writhing mob of horsemen, every rider burdened with at least one pistol and one carbine. Reflected lamplight struck against cartridge belts and only the constant remonstrances of Johnny Welker kept the angry talk to a minimum.

When Clint came up Welker went forward to meet him. " Everything's ready," he reported. " I put Benton and Custer where you wanted 'em and split the riders up into four posses. With all the comin' and goin' and noise and darkness I don't know exactly how many guns to each posse, but there are no less than thirty to each crew." Welker paused, peering down the roadway. " Is he gone?" he inquired.

Clint nodded, gazing past at the men. " Yes, he's gone. Did you tell them the plan, Johnny?"

" Benton and Custer did. They warned 'em too."

" About what?"

" Well; among other things about makin' a lot of noise or shooting first and looking afterwards—stuff like that." Welker's saturnine gaze switched to the milling horsemen in the roadway. " As if they didn't know about things like this," he concluded dryly. " Isn't a man-jack there hasn't been out with at least five posses, Clint."

" Hey," Custer called forth impatiently. " What's holding things up, Clint?"

" A small detail," answered the sheriff. " Somebody's got to ride out a ways and meet the hostages, Will."

For a brief moment the men were silent, then Carl Benton said quietly : " I'll do that. I'll ride ahead of my posse and scout them up and fetch them back to town."

Johnny Welker came forward leading two saddled horses. Clint accepted the reins to one animal and swung up. " All right, Carl," he called out. " But if anything goes wrong send riders to the other posses."

" What's going to go wrong?" Someone wanted to know, and Clint watched Johnny step across his mount before he answered.

" Like keeping the hostages," he said flatly. " Don't think for a minute those rustlers are dumb enough to turn them loose just because we released Amador."

A stony curse exploded in the night. There were echoes and variations to it until Clint held up his hand for silence.

" If they keep their word," he said, " fine. Only I don't think they will because they know perfectly well that they're safe from attack only as long as they have their hostages." From the corner of his eye he saw Will Custer draw taut in the saddle, staring at him.

" I think they'll keep our people until they cross the line," he concluded. " Now let's ride for it."

" Wait!" The newspaperman shouted, but Clint was already reining out, the racket of his posse drowning out Custer's repeated cry. " Wait, Clint! You can't do this!"

The moon, more whittled-down-looking than it had been the night before, cast earthward only enough light to make out immediate objects. Clint's body of horsemen loped steadily behind their leader. Dimly heard and diminishing was the cry of Will Custer. It was soon lost and for a number of miles Clint neither slowed nor looked around seeking familiar faces among his men.

More than an hour passed before Clint's riders slowed around him, bunching up and riding loosely southward. A rider eased forward to ride stirrup with the sheriff. It was Bruce Gollar, dark, swarthy face evil-appearing in that brooding gloom.

" You figure to jump them?" he asked.

" Not until I'm sure it can be done safely," Bruce was told.

" Then," said Gollar firmly, " you're going to have to go over the line."

This was not something Clint had not considered. It was illegal for any armed body of Americans to cross the Mexican border. This law was what had made it possible for raiders to successfully enter Texas, steal cattle and horses, kill Texans, and escape with impunity. Even U.S. troops could not cross the border without permission, and by the time permission had been secured in all cases to-date from the Mexican government, the brigands had disappeared. Clint had made up his mind hours earlier that if the possemen would follow him, and he never doubted but what they would, that he would cross over. He had told no one this, nor did he tell Gollar of his determination now, because he had opposed this identical idea when others had suggested it.

He rode along in bitter silence. It was hard for a strong man to do precisely what he had consistently refused to allow others to do and what he did not believe was right—and yet what he was now firmly resolved to do himself in violation of the law. It made it no easier, either, that he understood perfectly why he was willing to break the law now; Florence.

He did not try to answer the question of whether or not he would have been so willing to cross the line if Florence had not been among the hostages for the elemental reason that, being essentially a realist, he was not being called upon to make that decision.

But on the immediate issue he was fully resolved. He was going into Mexico!

" Who are the men with us?" he asked Gollar.

" Rangemen," Bruce said succinctly. " A few JM riders, some Quanah Buttes boys. All good men. Welker hand-picked 'em for this posse."

Clint nodded. Welker would have done that. He was a shrewd person.

" What was Mr. Custer all steamed up about?" Gollar asked.

" He didn't want anything done until the hostages were safely back in town."

Gollar considered this for a while then said : " It's pretty hard to know what's right sometimes. If we'd waited I reckon the hostages would've come back. The trouble with that is that the raiders'd have swung a wide loop and made us like it, which would have made them bolder than ever."

" Yeah."

" On the other hand——"

" I know," Clint said sharply, preferring not to discuss the alternative.

Gollar understood and grunted. Then he spoke on a

variation of the topic and this time Clint did not stop him. " The thing is, though, that sooner or later those fellers have got to be stopped from raiding up into Texas. Isn't a man, woman, or kid safe up here with them charging up here every month or so."

And that, in Clint's mind, was the crux of the thing. It was basically his reason for riding now with an armed body of Texans, determined to chase the marauders into Mexico if necessary in order to completely smash them. Florence actually was, for Sheriff Clint Verrill, the determining factor, but she had only tipped the scales, and as he rode along now, he wondered if he had not known all along that some day the Texans would have to break the letter of the law in order to protect themselves.

It relieved him a little to think this might be so, but the closer they got to the border the more pointed became his conviction that, compelled by necessity or not, what he was contemplating was definitely illegal.

The night was fully down; it was well past midnight before Clint stopped. He knew every foot of this great plain even without landmarks and knew exactly where he now was.

The line, marked at distant intervals by small stone monuments, lay less than five miles to the south. North and east lay the Travis cow country. West was an almost limitless run of prairie that broke eventually against the bony flanks of New Mexico's mountain ranges. South, for thousands of miles, was the broken country of Mexico. It was a land of deserts, mountains, drowsy and ageless villages, phlegmatic peasants and fierce brigands. Mexico was a land of the wildest contrasts; it was a cruel, crafty, sun-drenched land, and the mere sight of armed Texans had always brought forth from its people hatred and silence. Clint's posse could expect no help from the natives in their pursuit of the brigands; in fact they could expect bullets in the back if they were careless enough to let this happen.

"They ought to be on their way by now," a lanky rider opined. "Been about four hours since we left town."

Clint dismounted. The others followed his example. Mostly, being rangemen who spent the greater part of their lives apart from others, they were taciturn and patient. A few smoked, there was a little sigh of desultory conversation. Here and there a man stretched out full length with his hat for a pillow and drowsed.

Bruce Gollar came forward at Sheriff Verrill's beckoning. "We've been bearing west," Clint told the cowboy, "and somewhere along here is where they'll probably try to cross over. But it might be farther west so maybe we'd better detail a few men farther along. Pick four or five riders, have them string out a mile or so apart, and tell them to signal with a gunshot if they encounter a band of horsemen." As Gollar was turning away Clint added a precaution : "There's a chance they may not get down here before sun-up. Pass the word for everyone to pick a brush clump or a buffalo wallow to hide in."

"What about our horses?" Gollar asked.

There was nothing large enough to conceal a horse

for miles and Clint knew it. He shrugged. " We dassn't send them away so about all we can do is leave that up to each rider."

Gollar departed and Clint swung up. To the nearest men he said he was going on a short scout and rode north-west.

The day had been long and hot; now, as he rode away leaving behind the soft murmur of voices, swaying gently in his saddle beneath the stars, with the great depth of silence broken only by the grind of his mount's shod hoofs against powdery earth, he felt physically tired and mentally lethargic. There would be a fight. He knew that. If not here then somewhere else, but one way or another he would meet the outlaws who had Florence.

Dwelling for a time on the reaction of an Easterner who was in the hands of raffish Mexican brigands, he thought Florence would be more than ever embittered. She would have faced lawlessness in its rawest form. He made a cigarette, concealed the match inside his hat, inhaled and exhaled. It would be hard to face the reproach in her eyes when—and if—they met again. He envisaged that look of reproach; her reiteration of the things she had said about the West : It was crude : it was lawless; it was savage. And as usual he could feel what his reply might be but he could not form it into words.

Riding now down the long funnel of night, tired, feeling a little guilty over what he was determined to do if it proved necessary, a little disillusioned and therefore feeling close to defeat, he could recall quite vividly the high and low moments of his own life; of the environment which had hammered him into what he was. Beyond it, always present, was the firm vision of Florence's beauty; the inflections of her voice; her long silences and the upslanting quickness of her probing glance.

He punched out the cigarette on his saddlehorn and flung it down; made a strong effort to rally his strength, his strong resolve. Memory, he told himself, was a feeble light for a man to light his life with. It grew steadily feebler too as years passed. Sorrow was also something one endured but did not wallow in. He had lost Florence Berry. Nothing was going to change that. And the years before, the endless days which had shaped him into what he now was. Nothing could alter them either. So—they remained separated by ways of life neither could change; at least he couldn't change. Let it go at that; he had been deeply moved by a girl. Let it stop right there. Perhaps it might have been far better had he never known her. He wasn't sure of that, though. He wasn't even certain that if he had known in advance how it would end that he would not have gone ahead and enjoyed the short moments of pure pleasure anyway.

He drew upright in the saddle, sucked back a great lungful of air, halted his horse and strained for sound. There was nothing to hear; that fully dark night with its watery starshine was powerfully silent. He went on again, always bearing north and west because he felt the outlaws would be riding south from that direction.

Hours passed and a small doubt formed in his mind. He knew the raiders would not tarry along the way. He also thought they must be close by now—unless, as he had feared back in town, they had decided to flee in another direction. In either event he knew they would not get clear without a fight. But what troubled him was that, if they did not head south, straight for the border, one of the other posses would encounter them and above all else, he wanted to meet those outlaws himself.

He estimated the time finally, deduced it was close to dawn, and turned back. The Mexicans had either sought escape in some other direction or they were not hurrying. It occurred to him the latter might be the case. It also occurred to him that if it was, the marauders were deliberately taking their time because they did not fear being attacked—which meant simply that they had not released their hostages.

When he got back where the others were, Bruce Gollar met him with a saturnine expression. " Seems like we been out-foxed," the cowboy said.

Clint dismounted and stood hip-shot. " We won't know for another couple of hours," he replied. " Not until sun-up."

" Some of the boys are—"

A man upon the ground abruptly hissed for silence. They turned to regard him. He was lying prone with his ear pressed to the ground. After a moment he said : " Rider coming from the north-east."

Everyone grew very still. Moments later they distinctly heard the roll of hoofs. The men came up off the ground facing this new sound without speaking. When the rider was distantly visible as a swaying silhouette Bruce Gollar grunted aloud and spoke.

"Bob Stewart. I recognise his horse. He was with Benton's posse."

They pushed forward as the cowboy drew up in a sliding halt and flung down. "Sheriff," he said swiftly. "Carl sent me to tell you you was right—they didn't turn them folks loose."

"That ain't no news," a rider said dryly. "We figured that hours ago."

"He also said to tell you we picked up their sign an' tracked 'em out around Chavez Ravine, then straight south."

"They sure aren't in any hurry," Clint exclaimed, feeling both relieved that the brigands were coming to him, and fearful because they still had Florence. "Where is Carl now?"

"Him and them others are followin' the track as best they can. It's a mighty poor night for pickin' up sign. They got to ride pretty slow so as not to lose out."

"How many does Carl figure are in their band?"

"About fifty."

"Pretty big bunch," a cowboy said quietly. "A feller might make his wages yet tonight—if he can catch a few loose horses."

Someone chuckled.

Bruce Gollar stood thoughtfully frowning. After a moment he said to Clint: "While you were scouting I made a little sashay myself. I found fresh tracks headin' north. They weren't more'n a day or two old and I figure it's got to be our friends from south o' the border."

"Well," Verrill wanted to know. "What of it?"

"They'll more'n likely take the same trail back. They're familiar with it and they aren't in any position now to go exploring."

"Go on."

"We can ambush 'em."

"Any brush handy?"

"Lots of chaparral, Sheriff. I figure that's why they used that trail; it gave 'em pretty fair cover in case anyone was ridin' down this way and might've seen them."

Clint turned on his heel heading for his mount. "Let's go," he called over his shoulder and Benton's messenger joined the others.

Bruce Gollar led the way at a stiff trot. Just before they reached a faintly discernible trail through a thicket of thorny chaparral Gollar drew back beside Clint.

"Want me to send the boys we put out to the west?" he asked.

Clint said no; that as an added precaution they should be left where they were, then, when Gollar reined back and swung down the sheriff followed his example.

Gollar went ahead of his horse in a crouch until he found what he sought. He then pointed earthward. "There's the tracks, fresh as daisies. Some barefoot, some shod."

Clint was satisfied. He studied the terrain. If the

horses were led back half a mile and guarded there they might not be discovered. He detached four men to accomplish this and warned them against letting the animals nicker when they scented the Mexicans' mounts. Some of his possemen were reluctant to part with their mounts but no one openly protested. As the horses were being led away Clint called sharply to the guards. He then went forward, took down his lariat and told the other Texans to do likewise.

Bruce Gollar wagged his head over this but said nothing. It was as well that he didn't because Clint did not have in mind roping the outlaws as they passed; instead he took four of the ropes, tied them securely together, made one end of this snare fast to the base of a tough old bush, crossed to the far side of the trail and secured the other end to another chaparral clump. The rope was stretched taut no more than two feet off the ground and Gollar, with dawning understanding, laughed aloud.

"Might work at that," he said. "At least it'll sure dump the leaders."

Clint re-crossed the trail where the men stood. "These men have a woman with them. They also have three men who were on the stage too. You know what might happen if any of us try any sound shots."

They knew, and the fact that none of them asked any questions proved it. Several men checked their carbines and slapped hip-holsters. They all studied the brush thickets around them waiting for final instructions.

"String out," they were told. "Pick spots where you

can see the trail without being seen and don't fire until I do."

Clint remained in the middle of the trail as the men moved off and Gollar, watching him, paused. " You coming?" he asked.

Verrill shook his head. " I'll be back up the trail a ways," he answered. " I'm going to give them a chance to stay alive by surrendering."

Gollar swore. " They'll kill you," he exclaimed. " What have they got to lose?"

" When you're facing a gun, Bruce, you grab at straws. It makes no difference which side of the law you're on—you still make a pretty frantic effort to stay alive."

Gollar removed his hat, scratched his head, replaced the hat, jerked it forward and stalked off. There were all kinds of heroes in the world, he thought privately, but no more useless heroes than dead ones; all those Mexicans had to do was put a gun to Florence Berry's head and ride on—the sheriff would not dare try to stop them—then, in passing, they only had to fire one round and Travis, Texas, would be in the market for a new lawman. Bruce Gollar, a man of directness and forceful action, was not the first nor last Texan to underestimate Clint Verrill.

He burrowed into the brush near the spot where Clint finally took his stand some hundred feet north of the lariat-snare, and growled at the spiny thorns which gouged him. After settling low, carbine at the ready, he said pointedly : " Sheriff : you got any particular fellers in mind that'd make good pall bearers?"

E

Clint made no answer although he heard clearly enough. He was busy looping the remaining lariats into two very long ropes which he worked swiftly at tying at intervals northward along the trail utilising only the stoutest chaparral bushes as anchors. When he finished lacing the west side of his trap he made the second length of joined ropes fast along the east side, and for several hundred feet above the trip-rope the outlaw-trail was strongly roped off with hard-twist manila lariats not even the strongest horse could break.

When he finished he paused to catch his breath then walked back to stop where Gollar was watching and began to twist up a cigarette.

" What was that about pall bearers?" he asked.

" Nothing," the cowboy mumbled. " But if they don't believe they're in a trap you're still going to need 'em."

Chapter Four

SHORTLY BEFORE SUN-UP a call floated downwind and
Gollar said : " They're coming. You can still get in
here with me if you're a mind to."

Clint cradled his carbine, waiting. He did not answer
the cowboy. He was not thinking of the outlaws he
would confront, he was thinking instead of the look he
would find on Florence's face at sight of him.

" I hear 'em," Gollar volunteered, and after saying
that, the chaparral where he was secreted quivered
slightly as the cowboy raised his carbine, pushed it
carefully among the limbs, waiting.

Clint also heard oncoming riders. They were not
hurrying and only gradually did the jingle of rein-
chains, spur rowells and bit-crickets come musically
to him.

" Your last chance," Gollar hissed from the underbrush.

Moments later the first bandit appeared. He was a
short burly man with an enormous sombrero, a
swarthy face which was badly pock-marked, and
crossed bandoleers over his chest. He rode along loosely

and did not see the man afoot ahead of him until less than fifty feet separated them. Then he hauled back on the reins with an explosive curse and froze. Clint's snugged-back carbine was staring him in the face with its solitary dark eye socket. The Mexican was very still.

Other riders came on riding loosely and one called forward. " Challo; go on," he said in careless Spanish. " Is it that you are turned to stone, old one?"

" *Mira*," the unmoving *vaquero* said in reply, and might have said more but several other riders crowded up behind him and also stopped, struck dumb at the sight of a solitary Texan barring their path with a cocked, pointed carbine.

When the entire marauding party was halted a large, fair man pushed forward and stopped with both hands atop the saddlehorn. He gazed steadily at Sheriff Verrill for a long silent moment, then he smiled, reached up, thumbed back his hat and rolled his eyes. " You terrify us," he said in perfect English. " One lone man with his gun barring our way." The bandit leader's teeth flashed. " Tell me, *Señor;* do you have a wife? Little ones perhaps? It is too bad. *Gringas* make very handsome widows, no?"

Clint lowered the carbine, grounded it and leaned upon it. He also smiled. " The wives of *bandidos*," he answered in a strong tone, " make even better widows. Where are the hostages you promised to turn loose?"

The fair Mexican jerked his head backwards. " With us," he said simply. " That is why you killed your horse getting down here ahead of us?"

" My horse is far from dead. He is much fresher

than your own animal, *jefe*. Let me see that the *prisoneros* are unharmed."

The Mexican shrugged. " Pifas," he barked in Spanish to a nearby *vaquero*. " Have the *gringos Tejanos* brought forward. It is a small thing to grant a dying man's wish." His teeth flashed again in the uncertain light. " *Señor;* you are a brave man. I am sorry for what I must do. You realise that."

Clint ignored the bandit leader as Florence came forward on foot, walking ahead of three grim-faced men. At sight of Clint she stopped dead-still, staring. Her eyes went shades darker and her face paled. She would have run forward but a bandit carbine was thrust forward to stop her.

The chieftain watched with slow comprehension brightening his face. " Ah; I comprehend now," he murmured in soft Spanish, and made a slight bow toward Clint. Speaking again in English he seemed almost sympathetic. " A man in love is usually made brave, no? Well; I think we——"

" The border is less than five miles from here," Clint cut in to say. " You have an even chance of getting across alive, *jefe*—but only if you release the prisoners here and now."

The Mexican's brows went up. His eyes turned chilly. " You are threatening us, *Señor*? One lone *Tejano* threatens fifty *dorados*—fifty Golden Ones?"

Clint's next words fell into silence like iron chips. " Listen *jefe* : you are in a trap. Both sides of this trail are roped off. You can't break out of the brush. Hidden in the brush also, on both sides of you, there are thirty more *Tejanos*. Every one of them has a carbine trained on you right now." Clint's voice carried into the stillness. The Mexicans behind their chieftain began to probe the paling darkness with uneasy stares.

" You can take your choice : Turn the prisoners loose right now and surrender, or try and fight out of the trap." Verrill shook his head. " I don't think very many of your men will get away, *jefe*."

The bandit continued to stare down at Clint. He squinted his eyes and straightened slightly in the saddle. " I think you lie, *Señor*," he growled. " We saw no horses as we approached and I do not see either the ropes you spoke of or the men either." He lifted his left hand, the one holding his reins, as though to ride forward. Close behind him a Mexican spoke suddenly in a torrent of frightened Spanish.

" It is the sheriff from Travis," this last voice said, the words running all together. " It was he who released me from their jailhouse, *jefe*. He is a very formidable man; he does not lie."

" Shut up, Amador," the brigand leader snarled. " I wonder now that we ran this peril for so little of a man as you even though we are related." The rein-hand came down again. The greeny eyes turned glassily forward and fell upon Clint again. " *Señor;* if what you say is true it changes nothing because we still have our *prisoneros*. Go ahead; tell your *Tejanos* to fire." There was a blur of movement and the raider's fisted gun glistened in the pre-dawn. A solitary snippet of sound jarred loudly as the gun was cocked and brought to bear on the back of Florence Berry's head. " Well,

Señor Tejano? Why don't you tell your men to fire?"

"If I had wanted you dead I would have told them to fire when you first rode into the trap, *jefe*. I want the prisoners and I am going to have them."

"Dead or alive?"

Clint nodded. "Dead or alive," he repeated. "But if they die, believe me *jefe* you will go with them."

The Mexican stared hard at Clint. He made a soft but audible sigh. "Ahhhh; I think you mean it," he said, and eased off his pistol but did not holster it. "You *Tejanos* call this a Mexican Standoff don't you?"

"We do."

The rider shrugged. He did not appear in the least frightened, but his brow drew down in thought. For a while he said nothing, then: "And if I give you these people—what then?"

"You can ride out of the trap."

"Like that? So easily, *amigo*?"

"Like that. You have my word."

"Then I am bewildered. Why did you ride so hard to catch us? It was not necessary. We would have turned your people loose over the line."

"Maybe. But I think you're a liar. Anyway, it doesn't make any difference now. Just tell that man to lower his carbine, then turn around and ride out of here."

"One question," the Mexican said. "What happens after we ride out?"

"I told you before. It's only about five miles to the border."

" Ahhhh; I understand now. As long as we have not the prisoners your men will be able to chase us."

Clint answered both truthfully and grimly, leaving no room for doubt in the Mexican's mind what he intended once the hostages were safe. " Exactly. It is a sporting chance. I think it is better than what you had in mind for the hostages, too."

The Mexican scratched the tip of his nose with his pistol barrel. He frowned slightly. " You think I would have cut their throats?"

" Perhaps. I think it more likely you would have held them for ransom. It's happened before with raiders like you. Not often have the hostages come back alive." Clint hoisted the carbine off the ground, held it crossways in both hands with one finger on the trigger. " It's your choice," he said. " We've talked long enough."

The Mexican nodded. " *Si;* we have talked enough." He looked over his shoulder at the silent, listening riders behind him then faced Clint again. " I like better odds," he finally said. " I will give you the prisoners. You will give me a twenty minute start." Before Clint could reply he added : " No; I think I take the woman along as far as the border. She is very lovely. That way none of your men will overtake us. As you said—our horses are not fresh. If your mounts are stronger you could overtake us." He motioned to the Mexican standing in front of Florence. " Put her back on her horse, *muchacho.*"

" Wait a minute," exclaimed Clint. " You have my word about the twenty-minute start. Leave her here."

The Mexican smiled triumphantly. " *Señor;* I see where your heart lies. It is a good thing for us." He lifted his reins, holstered his pistol and spun his horse.

" Leave the other *gringos* with their friends," he ordered, and, throwing Clint a casual salute he began riding back the way he had come. Very slowly, with uneasy glances, his villainous riders followed after, none of them making any move toward their armament or urging their horses out of a walk.

Clint's expression was deadly. It stopped the released hostages from speaking when they got up close to him, and they too turned to watch the raiders ride off in silence.

Bruce Gollar pushed his way clear of the underbrush, went over to stand beside Clint and add his bleak stare to the others. Gradually, as the Mexicans passed, other Texans came forward until finally the entire posse was there in the empty trail.

" Get your lariats," Clint said eventually. " Bruce; have the horses brought up."

Gollar had a question framed on his lips but he did not utter it. Instead, he sent several of the men after their mounts then spoke to the three former hostages. For a while Clint's white-hot anger kept him aloof but after a few moments he crossed out of the trail where the hostages were, and listened.

Two of the prisoners were salesmen; one for a national firearms company, the other for a dry goods concern. The third man was a minister, one of the itinerant brotherhood of evangelists who toured the West preaching at every cowtown. Rangemen called them " sky pilots." It was the minister who was speaking when Clint came up.

" We were roughly handled," he was telling Bruce, " but I think only because they are rough men. The young lady—she was accorded more courtesy, but I think when they spoke of her it was with something evil in mind. They always spoke in Spanish about her, but men's expressions everywhere are the same. They are readable, gentlemen, and their expressions respecting her were very evil."

The gun salesman had more pointed and profane observations to make. Clint's Texans listened in stony silence until the horses came up, then the sheriff detailed Bob Stewart to remain with the released hostages because there were no extra horses, and wait until Benton's posse came up. It would be up to Benton, Clint told Stewart, to get the salesmen and minister back to Travis

He led his posse south without hurrying and the first mile there was very little conversation. Not until the sun came over the rim of the world to splash hard yellow light over everything did the men loosen in their saddles.

Southward the desert continued flat and sparsely brush-covered for several miles. Then the chaparral thickened, the land showed evidence of breaking up into shallow arroyos, and a long way off, smoke-hazed in the early daylight, great craggy mountains were visible. They were deep in Mexico with miles of open country between them and the Texans who were keeping steadily onward.

"He's pretty confident," Gollar said as they were riding along. "Look yonder." He pointed with his right hand.

The raiders were slightly more than a mile ahead. They were not riding swiftly but, as the cowboy had observed, seemed to have little fear the Texans would precipitate a fight. Five of them were fanned out in vidette-fashion around the main body, but all of the riders were lolling along in that relaxed and confident attitude which was normally associated with men who had nothing at all to fear.

Clint did not speak but his gaze never wavered nor softened. He was having difficulty with himself; having thoroughly made up his mind to cross the line earlier, it was hard now to decide against that course providing the bandit leader kept his word and released Florence at the border. He wanted to smash the marauders and in his mind he found ample support to excuse his wish to chase them down into Mexico.

If the outlaws released Florence at the line, and if he stopped there in accordance with international law, a precedent would have been established. In every *cantina* on the Mexican side of the line brigands would celebrate the discovery of a way in which raiders could withdraw safely from Texas, and the very thing he was determined to stamp out—rustler-raids into Texas— would increase and flourish.

Additionally, the brigand leader of the band who had Florence would become a great hero to his people. The next time he raided up into Texas he would not come with fifty rustlers, he would have a hundred, perhaps two hundred, and he would take hostages wholesale. Not only that, Clint told himself, but the next time he would not be so easy to trap and finally, he would not release the women.

On the coin's other side, if Clint went over the line after Florence was released, Mexico's officials would raise a great cry; would accuse Texas of invading Mexico and U.S. troops would come swarming down after Clint's men. As Clint had warned the cowmen back in Travis; such an invasion might even spark a war between the two countries. He was certain that whatever happened the Texans who went with him would be tried as filibusters if taken by U.S. troops, and if apprehended by the Mexicans would be lined up and shot in accordance with Mexican law, which termed all foreign invaders taken in arms, as " pirates."

He did not hit upon what he considered the only solution until they were less than a mile from the line : He would send his posse back and continue on into Mexico alone. He would send Florence back with the men.

He had only just thought of this when Bruce scattered his thoughts with a hard curse. " Better hold up," the cowboy growled to Clint, and the sheriff raised his arm halting the men around them.

The Mexicans were astraddle of the line and they too had stopped, obviously looking back, watching the Texans. Slightly more than half a mile separated the two parties. Clint could distinguish Florence very easily. He also had no trouble making out the brigand chieftain; he was lolling in his saddle smoking. It was clear too that whatever he was saying amused his companions for a ripple of laughter carried easily in that sparkling, clear air.

"I'd like to get my hands around his gullet," Gollar snarled.

Behind Clint a tall, rangy rider made a cigarette with his reins looped and his calm, cold gaze running down the land in a direct and uncompromising way. "I kind of got a notion," this man said, "that Pancho there never had no idea at all about turning loose that girl."

An older rider, whose expressionless face was all the more deadly for its impassivity, spoke up. "If he don't I got a feeling it'll be the biggest mistake of his life." He paused a moment joining with the others in watching the brigands, then he drawled : "You know fellers, Benton's crew'll be coming up pretty soon, and it seems an awful waste to me, when there's all of us down here now, not to sort of jog over the line there and put an end to this raidin' business once and for all."

There was a unanimous murmur of approval from the possemen. Bruce Gollar slanted a surreptitious glance at the sheriff's face but could read nothing there. Clint was watching the Mexicans with no clear indication on his face of what lay in his mind.

"Well," someone said plaintively after several minutes more had passed, "if they're going to turn her loose, what're they waiting for anyway?"

There was an answer to this in every man's mind but none of them offered it.

The Mexicans seemed to be enjoying their role; the sombreroed leader continued to smoke and regard the Texans for some time. Then he dropped his cigarette, whirled his horse, gave a sharp order and the band lifted their horses into a steady lope riding southward. They were taking Florence with them into Mexico !

" I expected that," a Texan said sharply, and swore Clint's eyes, nearly black behind their narrowed lids, held fire points of wrath. He eased his mount over into a gallop with the Texans behind him. As they rode southward towards the line someone called out thinly : " Hey; there's a bunch of riders coming up behind us."

Clint twisted for a look. All he could clearly discern in the brilliant sunsmash was a rapidly moving dust-cloud. Straightening around he said to Gollar. " Benton I expect," and received a loud affirmative grunt in reply.

They were nearing the little stone border-markers when Clint saw the Mexicans halt and swing back to watch the Texans approach the line. It was easy to tell from their attitudes that they were prepared to enjoy watching their pursuers halt at the line.

Clint slowed his horse with the border less than a thousand yards onward. The men around him followed suit but there were some sharp queries called forward.

" Go on, Sheriff."

" What you stoppin' for?"

" Listen," Clint said loudly. " You boys go on back. We can't all cross the line."

Bruce Gollar bent a savage look at the sheriff. " You figuring to go on across?" he asked.

Clint nodded. " Alone," he replied. " This is personal fight from here on. Now you boys—"

Gollar threw back his head, emitted a chilling Comanche war-cry, and hooked his horse hard. The animal, startled as much by the yell as by the spurring, sprang ahead and hit hard in a furious run.

Men streamed past the sheriff yelling and brandishing carbines. He called to them; he yelled orders and even tried to swing his mount sideways in a blocking endeavour. All to no avail; the Texans raced up to the line and over it, never slowing, not even looking down as they passed from their own country into Mexico.

Clint was swept along with them but he was no longer in the lead. Still, he had no difficulty seeing the consternation which galvanised the Mexicans into abrupt action, inspiring them to lose their earlier confidence and inertia.

Raiders broke away from the main band quirting their horses hard, yelling to one another to flee for their lives, riding low over the necks of their mounts, and behind them, gaining swiftly on fresher horses roared the Texans.

Gunshots erupted : dirty little puffs of smoke rose into the morning air. Some of the outlaws tried shooting backwards but generally the brigands were concerned only with flight. The first raider fell after jerking fully upright in his saddle, flinging up his arms, then tumbling backwards off his horse. The second one, hard hit, made a wild grab at the mane of his horse, missed and went off sideways to bump along over the ground for no less than twenty feet before he came to a sprawled stop. A Texan's plunging horse leapt this man easily, but in so doing spoiled his rider's aim at another brigand.

Clint did not fire. He had his carbine up and cocked but he was straining to locate the brigand who was leading Florence's horse. Thickening dust made it nearly impossible to locate this man until he was sufficiently up with his companions to make out individual bandits. Even then, though, he did not at once see that Florence's guardian was heading away from his friends, making a break for what appeared to be a particularly dense chaparral thicket off to the east. What captured and held his attention finally was the fact that Florence's mentor kept the two mounts close together. They were the only riders who had not scattered.

Urging his horse to its utmost Clint streaked past several of the foremost Texans and caught up finally with Bruce Gollar. The dark man raised his arm to point ahead, temporarily diverting Clint from the pair of racing horses he had been watching. The brigand leader, evidently in an attempt to rally his men, was yelling at the top of his voice and making frantic arm-gestures. Some of the men, perhaps twenty or thirty of them, drew in closer to the main party. In this fashion they fled in a body, but also because of their bunching up in this fashion several were immediately cut down.

When Clint looked around again he could no longer

see Florence and her captor. They had vanished into the brush as completely as though they had never existed.

The pursuit slowed finally when Clint was able to get the attention of his men. There was some yelling, some gesticulating, which brought back the foremost riders. The men milled around Clint, their horses both winded and excited.

" One of them," Clint called out, " took off into the brush with her. Let the others go."

With a bound he set his horse towards the chaparral, burst through the first thorny wall of grey leaves and wiry limbs and struck a narrow game trail. Loping along he watched for intersecting trails and tracks. He did not find the latter until, a half hour later with the sun scorching both men and animals, he came out of the underbrush upon a slight rise. Then he found the tracks. However, before he had gone more than a mile onward a cowboy who was following a paralleling ridge, yelled excitedly : " Yonder they go !" And without ascertaining exactly who the man had seen the Texans set their horses into another long run.

They swept down into a long valley, crossed it and breasted a second rise. Beyond this one, with an adobe village clearly visible on their right, and farmed fields beyond the village, they saw their prey. But the two straining horses were no longer alone; around them were no less than fifteen other brigands.

As Clint rocketed forward he deduced that the outlaws who had split off from the main band had come swiftly to recognise their best course to safety was to

F

go with the man who had the *gringa;* the *norteameri-cano* girl. Here at least, with her as hostage, they might be able to save their lives.

It was a grim race and as the horses of both parties tired under that blasting sun it became even grimmer. The Texans rode in total silence, their eyes never leaving the men they were pursuing. The brigands, on the other hand, were equally as determined to make good their escape and urged their animals on even after they began to falter badly.

"Not much longer," Clint told his men. "Their horses are about done for."

"If they'd slow down," someone said, "we could talk to them. Let 'em go after they give up the girl."

A hoarse voice sounded off in dissent. "I'm not for lettin' the whelps go even after we get the girl. We've come this far—no sense in turnin' back now short of layin' a few of them out for Final Rites."

This voiced opinion met with nearly unanimous agreement. It was obvious also, that the brigands up ahead knew how the Texans felt; even after they were compelled by the condition of their mounts to stagger along in a caricature of a gallop, they showed them-selves grimly determined to keep on.

Bruce Gollar, studying the countryside, asked if any one knew what lay ahead. There were several vague references to towns farther along, but no one was familiar, it turned out, with the immediate locality.

Clint, who had been seeking to guess why the brig-ands were bearing in their present direction instead of southerly after their leader, came to the conclusion that the outlaws were striving to reach a village, perhaps even a large town where troops were garrisoned, but at least some place where they could secure aid and possibly reinforcements. Believing this, he told Gollar to take the men whose horses were standing up best and try to get around the outlaws. As Gollar and some twelve other Texans out sharply on ahead the brigands surmised their intention and fell to gesturing excitedly to one another.

They held to their easterly course, however, until Gollar's men were nearly abreast of them to the south, then swung abruptly northward making for the broken, rocky country on their left. As they made this change of direction Clint sighted Florence. Her long hair was flying loose and it was obvious even at that distance from the way she clung with both hands to the saddle-horn, she was near collapse from strain and exhaustion.

The first brigands faded beyond sight where an arroyo loomed. Other raiders also dipped down into this cover. All them then clattered up the far side making for higher country.

Gollar's men, swinging northward also, were the closest Texans. They gave the Mexicans no rest but pressed them hard forcing them to expend their horses. A few gunshots erupted when Clint's party came up and Bruce came forward to meet the sheriff with a sweat-shiny face.

" They've dismounted up in the rocks," Gollar reported. " I think we got another Mexican Standoff. We dassn't charge 'em and they still got the girl."

Clint said nothing, but walked his spent animal close to the arroyo's near bank and sat there gazing ahead into that wild and stony country where the brigands had been brought to bay. When the Texans came up, mostly afoot leading their animals, bared guns glinting sharply in the sunlight, he said : " Easy, boys. I think they know they've played out their string. Let's not push them into something we'll all regret."

A brigand hoisted his carbine from behind a stunted pine tree. A soiled white neck-cloth waved dismally in that windless midday air from the gun-barrel.

" All right," Clint called. " We'll hold fire."

The Mexican stepped gingerly into sight. He stood a moment knee-sprung, ready to instantly leap back behind the tree. When no shots came he drew up a little, but he presented no very brave nor confident appearance.

" We will give you the woman," he said, enunciating English words with painful clarity. " You will ride away then."

Clint agreed instantly. " We will ride away. Now send her over."

From off on the Mexican's right, low in some underbrush, someone hissed angrily in Spanish. The brigand spokesman listened briefly, sought to argue, then shrugged and faced forward again. " One more thing," he called uneasily. " We need three horses to replace those we can no longer ride. You must give them us or we will keep the girl."

Before Clint could reply an angry Texan stepped up to the very brink of the arroyo and swore fiercely at the Mexicans. " You send that girl out here right now, you lyin' devils, or we're coming up in there after you!"

Clint reached forward, caught the Texan by the arm and spun him around. " Mister," he drawled icily, " the next time you pull something like that you're going to wake up stretched out on the ground."

" Sheriff!" The angered Texan exclaimed in loud protest. " If we give up three horses that means three of us got to try and walk back out of here. You know cussed well those devils'll have the countryside roused against us. Hell; we'll be doin' real good if we get out of this alive—*with* our horses."

Gollar stepped forward. " He's right, Clint. We only got about a third of their crew bottled up here. The others'll be ridin' among the villages rousin' the people against us. They might even stir up the Mex army. We got to get the girl and streak it out o' here."

Beyond, at the outer edge of gunshot, the Mexicans too were arguing among themselves. Clint could only catch an occasional word but he heard enough to understand that the outlaws meant to let Florence go, then trail the Texans sniping as they rode along, in this fashion hoping to delay their departure from Mexico until either the other brigands came up or the rural, Mexican constabulary troops arrived.

He pushed past both Bruce Gollar and the other Texan to call out. " Send the girl over," he commanded. " We will give you no horses. If you don't send her over we will kill every one of you."

The Mexicans argued furiously among themselves;

it was not difficult to hear their raised voices either. Three or four were for fighting it out. One suggested killing Florence. The majority though, insisted that their prisoner be sent across to the Texans. They prevailed in the argument finally by pointing out that the Texans had crossed the line, which proved they were very resolute, very formidable men, and would clearly keep their word about killing the outlaws. One *gringa* they stoutly maintained, was far from an equivalent for fifteen Mexican lives.

Florence appeared out of the underbrush. She was pushed roughly forward, stumbled, caught herself and paused to lean upon a huge boulder. Clint called for a canteen and when it was brought he started forward, crossed the arroyo, paced strongly forward into the sights of every crouching brigand, and came at last to Florence's side. He gave her the canteen, held it while she drank, then, with an arm around her waist, started back. He spoke softly, encouragingly, and although she made no answer he could feel her stride firming up.

They got to the arroyo, went down into it and laboured up the far side. Florence was panting; each breath was an effort but she struggled onward and Clint continued to whisper soft encouragement.

A dozen bronzed hands reached forward to help them up the arroyo's near side. Then Florence collapsed. Clint caught her, lifted her bodily and walked with sweat nearly blinding him, to the shade near the horses. There, he put her down gently, accepted Bruce's neck-cloth, soaked it in water and bathed her face.

Around him, and farther back along the arroyo, his

men stood in deep and savage silence. Into this hush came a Mexican's call.

"Hey, *gringos;* you got the woman. Now you ride off, eh?"

No one replied.

Bruce Gollar waited until Florence was sufficiently recovered to sit up, before he spoke. He did not miss the long glance which passed between the girl and the sheriff.

"My horse can stand a little extra weight so I'll carry her double the first few miles," he said. " Clint; we'd better be movin' along."

Words were piled up behind the sheriff's teeth but there was no time now for the kind of things he longed to say. He handed Florence up behind Bruce, mounted his own horse, cast a final look backwards where the Mexicans were still hidden from sight, then led off over the back-trail.

The weary, dust- and sweat-stained body of Texans rode ploddingly westerly paralleling the badlands where their earlier prey also rode abreast of them, but well beyond gun range and out of sight in the breaks, ravines, and tumbled profusion of the badlands, slipping along like jackals on their exhausted horses hoping for something to happen to the Texans which would give them an opportunity to attack the invaders and achieve vengeance.

Clint knew they were there; he was unfamiliar with this south-of-the-border country but he knew Mexicans as well as did any Texan and he shared the sectional distrust of them. They would snipe and harrass as soon as they were sure the Texans would not turn on them; until their time arrived they would skulk patiently along.

It was a long hour's ride before they got back to the last rise they had crossed earlier. There, they halted briefly to rest their horses again.

The land as far as anyone could see, was empty, but Clint had a presentiment and called up Bruce Gollar. " Scout ahead," he said. " Benton's posse can't be too far from here. But keep an eye peeled; I've got a feeling we're not going to ride back to Travis this easy."

Gollar handed Florence to another man and jogged off down the slope, crossed an intervening narrow little valley and pushed uphill on the far side to top out over the next rise.

Clint waited until Gollar was well on his way before leading the balance of the posse forward. He had not progressed more than five hundred feet when a solitary loud gunshot shattered the hush and every man with Clint drew up sharply and reached for weapons.

Bruce was spinning down off the far ridge in a long lope. As he rode he flagged frantically for Clint to lead off to the north into the badlands. Clint did so immediately and every man around him followed his example.

Chapter Five

STRIKING DEEP INTO the *pedregal*—rough, stony, lava-rock country—Clint's party came almost at once upon the astonished brigands who had been following them. There was a swift exchange of gunfire then the bandits fled. Their escape was facilitated by stunted junipers and pines, as well as by man-high boulders which lay at random between the arroyos and ravines. But the Texans, more earnestly seeking shelter for themselves than in attacking their enemies right at that moment, did nothing more than fire off a few rounds to expedite the brigands' departure.

Clint ordered his men to dismount, find cover for their animals, and take protective positions. He then went forward to meet Bruce Gollar. When the cowboy loped up and reined down, he called forward : " The rest of the band is just over that ridge. One of them saw me and tried a long shot."

" All of them?" Clint asked.

" Yeah; and maybe a few cousins and brothers as well. I didn't more'n make a darned quick estimate but I'd say there are at least seventy-five of 'em, and they're coming too . . ." Gollar looked over his shoulder then faced forward critically studying the *pedregal*. "Looks like a good place to hold 'em off," he said.

"Hold them off hell," Clint growled. "We've got to get out of here. It's a cinch they've sent for troops. Did you see anything of Carl's posse?"

"No. But then I didn't spend much time lookin' either."

The two men rode back into the broken country side by side, dismounted and handed their mounts over to a waiting posseman, then crawled atop a large rock to watch and wait.

It was not a very prolonged vigil. The brigands appeared atop the far rise, milled briefly then began the descent. It was obvious to the Texans they were following Gollar's tracks and when they hit the lowlands they swung north in a ragged cavalcade. Clint searched out the outlaw leader and found him when the brigands drew up in a jamming halt near some pines and catclaw clumps. He pointed him out to Gollar. The cowboy stared dourly for a time, then grunted.

"Out of range," he said. "When he gets close enough we better use him up. If he's out of it I figure the others'll slope."

Clint had already considered this, but the more he watched the renegades the less evidence he saw of their chieftain exposing himself. He was afoot among the horses giving orders and from the way his men moved off Clint became convinced that he had, sometime in his lifetime, been a soldier—probably a *pronunciamiento*, one of those perennial troublemakers who plagued

Mexico with constant revolutions. He said nothing of this to Gollar, but twisted on the rock to peer behind them where the Texans were crouching. He sought Florence but did not find her; some of his men had obviously seen that she was put safely out of harm's way. He considered the few men he could see, obviously with something in mind, then swung forward again and spoke to Bruce Gollar.

" Listen; you see what's happening out there?"

" Sure; he's splitting his force into two parties."

" Right; our *jefe*—our chief—is no fool. He's played this game before, Bruce. He's going to send those two columns around us on both sides, have them join somewhere behind us—and have us boxed in."

Gollar was unimpressed. " I've whipped my share of pepper-bellies before," he exclaimed grimly. " So has every man with us. We can bust out any time you give the word."

" We'd lose men," the sheriff explained. " But even if it was just us, I might be willing to try it."

" I understand," the cowboy said quietly.

" Then go get your horse, Bruce, sneak out the back way, cut around the badlands and go after Benton's posse."

Gollar's dourness vanished. He drew up a little off the rock. " Sure," he exclaimed. " Why didn't I think of that." He started inching backwards down off the boulder. Just before he struck the ground and started away the sheriff told him to be careful; that they would be unable to send out another man after they were surrounded and everything depended upon his reaching Carl Benton and bringing him back. Instead of offering any reassurance Gollar simply smiled and winked.

In front of Clint's rock the brigands were breaking up into their separate bands and beginning to angle forward. For a space of ten minutes there was scarcely a sound, then a carbine cracked beyond sight, off to Clint's right, and Sheriff Verrill knew their foemen were within range. He slid down off the rock and ducked into the underbrush seeking his companions.

Westerly somewhere, beyond sight, sunlight spilled slantingly against rough-cut ridges and arroyos. There was a deepening redness to its glow indicating that more than half the day was spent. Where Clint came to an opening he could look upwards beyond the trees and see where the sky was cut crossways with a thousand sharp splinters of that refracted light. Until then he had given no thought to time's passage. Now, compelled to face this new condition, he stood briefly wondering whether nightfall would help or hinder, his posse.

Hot silence fell. There was no gunfire. It was an uneasy time for the Texans and one arose from the forage grass to ask Clint where the brigands were. " Coming in at us from the east and west," he was told. " Slip around and warn the others to keep a sharp watch."

To the rear, back where the horses were or beyond, a woodpecker began his staccato beating upon a pinesnag. The sound rocketed in waves filling everyone's head with its harshness. Clint started to search for Florence; he knew how frightened she must be and although he could spare her no more than a moment, he wanted to reassure her; to look into her face and perhaps lay a hand upon her shoulder.

He did not get the chance. A posseman lying prone beside a craggy granite upthrust caught his attention with a small hand-wave and motioned Clint in closer. As the sheriff crouched low the Texan, his head pressed close to the ground so that he could see beneath the scanty underbrush, patted the earth with one hand. Clint went down beside him. In a whisper so soft it was scarcely audible the posseman said : " Off to the right a little and dead ahead. Three of 'em comin' on. They've taken their spurs off. See them?"

Clint saw nothing at first; not until one of the brigands glided through a patch of filigreed sunlight. " I see one of them," he husked.

" Keep watching," he was told. " The other two're with him." The Texan was briefly silent, then he said : " If those *hombres* are advancin' in line then the rest of 'em must be just about up to us too." He inched his carbine forward very carefully. " Pretty soon now somebody's goin' to get a big surprise—I hope it isn't us."

Clint said nothing. He was concentrating on the advancing brigands and had little difficulty, once he knew where to look, in finding the other two. The foremost Mexican, however, seemed to be experienced in this type of work. Probably, Clint thought, he had been appointed an advance scout. The man advanced in starts, never straightening up out of a crouch. He held his carbine across his body in both hands and constantly moved his head from side to side; he seemed to rely as much on his nose as his eyes to warn him of peril. From time to time he would grow motionless, head up and eyes nearly closed as though keening the still, hot air.

Clint was fascinated by the man's thoroughness. When the brigand angled south-east heading with extreme caution directly for the upthrust which hid Clint and his posseman, the sheriff reached back very slowly, drew out his six-gun, eased it forward and held it low, his thumb resting on the hammer. To the man beside him he whispered : " Is there anyone on ahead of us?"

" No. I crept out this far alone. The others are off to the right or farther back."

Clint was pleased. He had it in mind to take the brigand scout alive if possible. " Don't shoot until I do," he said, and began worming backwards into the shadows of the boulder which hid them. Once hidden from sight he cut silently around the rock, crawled on hands and knees to the protective cover of a further granite jumble, pressed his face against warm stone and peered out through a crack. The three Mexicans were standing motionless behind a chaparral bush peering through, evidently waiting to catch movement. Clint waited until they started forward again then, because they were quite close now and the least noise would alert them, he inched forward a foot at a time smoothing the way as he went so that no twigs would break under his weight. Sweat ran off him in rivulets. He stopped finally where the pile of rock sloped down into the earth, his heart sounding loud in his ears, wiped perspiration from his forehead and very carefully, an inch at a time, drew up off the ground. Beyond his place of concealment sounded the faintest rasp of leather over gravel; it served to orient Clint to the exact location of the brigands. He continued to straighten up and when at last he could see over, the outlaws were no more than ten feet past him.

He lay his pistol atop a shoulder-high boulder and without raising his voice, said gently : "*Alto!* Halt; don't open your mouths!"

The Mexicans turned to stone. The leader or foremost scout whipped upright to stand rigidly as though stung, but neither he nor his petrified companions made so much as a sigh.

"Bend forward and put down your guns. Don't drop them!"

Clint's prisoners obeyed, then drew back upright awaiting his next command. He edged around into full view, approaching from the rear, and with prods of his pistol barrel herded the captives over where the posseman who had first sighted the brigands was waiting with a broad smile.

"Saw the whole thing," he said softly to Clint. "Went off like clockwork. Now what?"

"Gag them," the sheriff ordered, "and pull off their boots." The Texan looked round-eyed. Clint pointed earthward with his gun-barrel. "'Take cast-iron bare feet to try and run away over this ground," he explained.

When the captives were effectively silenced and

stripped of their footgear Clint sent them back with the posseman to be put under guard of the Texans farther back.

After the prisoners and their guard were gone Clint retrieved the guns his captives had left, went back into the shadows of the rocks again, and sat down. He longed for a cigarette and a drink of water both, but these cravings were minor; an appraisal of the sky showed that evening was not far off. Speculating on the distance Bruce Gollar might have to traverse before he located Carl Benton, and the fact that nightfall might come before the brigands attempted a concerted attack, encouraged Clint to think that one event or the other might save his posse yet. He knew that Mexicans, like Indians, did not fight at night unless they were forced to. They might even be able to escape after dark, he speculated. By now their horses were recovered from the morning's gruelling chase.

It was a hope, but no more than that, for he had no sooner turned to watching the westerly approaches again then a fusillade of gunfire broke out far behind him to the east. Listening closely, he concluded that no surprise had been effected. It was not difficult to tell Mexican gunshots from the return-fire of his Texans. Mexican gunpowder, called by frontiersmen " coal dust," was really little more than that; it frequently did not explode at all or when it did it burnt slowly, smoked greatly, and each report was a deepthroated, thumping sound rather than an equivalent to the sharper, cleaner ' crack ' of Texan shots. In this case the reports were about equally divided indicating that the possemen had not been taken unawares.

He wanted to go toward the rising sounds of battle but did not do so; remembering the brigand leader's bold, wily face, he considered diversionary tactics on his part quite likely. Nor was he wrong, but in the interim the Texan who had led away the captives came darting forward to drop down beside Clint, panting.

"They made a drive on our horses," he said, speaking swiftly, excitedly. "They did it on horseback though and the boys heard them coming and were waiting."

Clint cocked his head, listening. The gunfire was slackening. He turned forward again. "Where is the girl?" he asked, and the cowboy, understanding, said strongly that she was safely hidden in the rocks and that the possemen were guarding her. He stretched out upon the ground, moved his head slowly seeking movement, then spoke again.

"I saw her for a minute. She asked about you."

Again Clint held his silence.

Suddenly the cowboy stiffened his full length and hissed. "They're coming!" He had time for no more than that.

Clint dropped low pushing forward his carbine. He too saw the shadows fading and swelling, moving up nervously but resolutely, sunlight's red glow upon their backs, upon their filled bandoleers and steel rifle-plates. It was like the advancing first units of an army, Clint thought, and felt suddenly both exposed and alone. They would need help and need it fast. "Fire!" he

said. " Make a racket that'll bring the others out here."
He did not wait for the cowboy to comply but raised
his own carbine and levered off three fast shots. At
once a burst of erratic gunfire came back, none of it
accurate and only a few bullets even travelling in the
right direction.

Pungent gunpowder-aroma hung in the afternoon
air, acrid-smelling and hazy. The brigands, experienced in the ruses necessary when men fired powder
which left tell-tale smoke, moved constantly after firing. At Clint's side the Texan said : " I got me one,"
and emptied his carbine, brought forth his hand-gun
and resumed firing. Clint reached back for the guns he
had taken from the captives and pushed them forward.

This sudden concerted, grim firing was too much for
the outlaws; some of them began to withdraw. A few,
less fearful and more determined, hunkered down behind trees and rocks to pin Clint and his companion
down. There were cries and curses in Spanish; there
were shouted taunts and grisly promises in bad English too, as the fight became a siege. Clint had no time
to consider anything but the men across from him in
the fading red afterglow of late afternoon. He was
unaware that succour had arrived until a brisk and
swelling fire broke out north of him where there was
considerable cover.

The Mexicans stopped cat-calling and settled down
to fighting. Clint risked a look from his natural granite
fortress but saw no one on his right. It did not matter;
in fact it was a good thing that he could not see the

Texans because if they had been exposed the Mexicans too could have seen them. He was immeasurably warmed by their presence, which was enough anyway.

The brigands began withdrawing. Occasionally a figure showed for a twinkling then disappeared. Clint fired often, not hopeful of hits but content to expedite the flight of his enemies.

Silence came gradually to replace the pandemonium. Clint reloaded his weapons and counted the empty loops in his shell-belt. If the others had no more ammunition than he had, they would be able to withstand only another two or three brushes. A lanky, dishevelled Texan crawled laboriously over the shale to come in behind Clint's rock rampart. He was sweat-streaked and filthy, but widely smiling.

" I reckon that'll hold 'em," he said, drawing up a little, leaning back against the boulder and peering ahead where grey smoke lingered among the trees and brush clumps. " Another hour or so and it'll be dark."

Clint, casting a look skyward, found that more time had passed than he had expected. He drew up off the ground, brushed dust off his shirt and began making a cigarette. " Any sign of Gollar or Benton?" he asked.

The lanky Texan wagged his head. " I ain't seen any," he replied. " But then I wasn't particularly lookin' either. This kind o' work keeps a man sort o' busy just makin' sure some greaser don't slip up behind him." He jerked his head sideways. " Some of the boys got a little jerky back yonder in the thicket. They sent me up here to relieve you if you're hungry."

"Jerky only makes a man thirstier," Clint said, lighting up, taking smoke deep into his lungs and letting it out slowly.

"They got water too. Got their canteens full. Go on," the posseman urged. "I'll spell you off for a while."

Clint went back, located the others with no trouble and found them in high spirits over having repulsed both brigand attacks. They greeted him quietly, offered him canteens of water and strips of jerked beef, some of it smoke-cured, some of it salt-cured.

"Where's Miss Berry?" he asked, and the men nodded towards a great jumble of rocks far back in the pines behind them.

"'Couple o' the boys are with her," a Texan drawled. "We got guards out in every direction." The man cocked a speculative eye skyward before speaking again. "You figurin' on pullin' out when it's dark, Sheriff?"

Clint was moving off when he replied. "Yeah; better check the horses and double the guard around them. *Jefe* Pancho'll guess we're going to try that."

Florence had in some mysterious way managed to scrub her face and comb her hair. She saw Clint coming and went forward to meet him. They did not speak at once but went side by side through the quickening haze of evening as far as a lonely place where tree-squirrels chattered scoldingly at them from overhead pine limbs and sank down there upon a cushion of needles. Summer's spotless sky was a backdrop for the sinking sun and heat hung over everything with its formless, lethargy-producing substance giving greater depth to the silence, and also to the mood which came now to settle over the lawman.

He was conscious of her closeness, of the long look she was putting on him, and of her silence. He picked up a twig and snapped it, the old incoherence coming forth to plague him; he did not, however, intend this time to offer excuses for his world as he had always sought to do before. He did not feel they would be adequate here, with raider guns encircling them somewhere in the near distance, so instead he said, "I expect it was pretty awful, wasn't it?"

"It was frightening," she agreed. "But I think the worst part was the running. They never remained long in one place." She made a rueful smile. "I am not used to riding like that." Her gaze was soft on his lowered profile. "I was astonished to see you standing there in their path alone, Clint. I almost fainted : I was sure they would shoot you."

"It was a chance," he said. "But I'll tell you something about Mexicans most folks don't understand. Sure; they'll kill men as quickly as anyone else. Maybe quicker. But they like to talk. If you can get a Mexican talking before he pulls his gun you aren't really in much danger. Of course you've got to have something worthwhile to say." He looked up finally. "How did they treat you, Florence?"

Her faint, soft smile heightened the smallest bit. "I suppose as well as anyone could have expected under the circumstances, Clint. The one you released . . ."

" Amador. Francisco Amador."

" Yes. The others call him Pancho."

" That's their nickname for anyone named Francisco," he told her. " In Texas folks call just about any Mexican Pancho. It's a pretty common name."

" He was very kindly towards me, Clint. He also told them that you were a dangerous man. I did not understand their talk exactly but I gleaned enough to get that much."

He smiled mirthlessly. " I reckon they weren't much impressed," he said, and gestured with one hand. " They've got us pretty well pinned down in here." He dropped the hand. " Florence; we're going to make a break for it after dark. Can you stand another hard ride?"

With no hesitation she said : " Yes; whenever you're ready, Clint."

He squirmed, picked up another twig and examined it closely. " I expect Texas is all you've always said it was, Florence. Bleak and cruel and savage . . ." He dropped the twig. " I won't apologise for it."

" You never have apologised for it, Clint."

" No; but just the same—"

" Why should you?"

" Why should I?" he said, surprised at her tone and look, at a complete loss to interpret her meaning or find the right words in that moment.

" Yes. Why should you feel it necessary to apologise for yourself or for the men in here with us? You're all Texans. You all broke international law by charging down here after those raiders. You did it to save me;

why should brave men have to apologise for doing what they believe to be right?"

"Well," he said, groping again. "Like I told you, Florence; Texas has come a long way in the last fifty years and it'll likely go still further in the next fifty years." His voice strengthened. "Meanwhile; folks are called on to do things they think are right—but others might think differently." He made a face. "I'm not telling it very well but maybe you'll understand."

"I understand, Clint," she told him softly. "I wouldn't want to have to learn every lesson in this fashion but I understand, believe me. Texans are a special kind of people. I said that to you once before, only then I meant it differently. I see things now that escaped me before. I want you to know that."

He mulled over her words beginning to hope, yet fearful too.

She reached forth, lay her hand over his and remained silent. In the gathering dusk her face was pale in its breadth, its strength, and shadows lay across it to conceal the deepening darkness of her gaze.

"Did you know he did not intend to set me free?" she asked.

He shrugged and continued silent a moment. "I thought he might not before I saw him. Afterwards, I was sure he didn't intend to."

"Was that what made you ride so hard to head him off?"

"Not exactly, Florence." He checked himself, not sure this was the truth. "Well," he said, starting over again. "Maybe that was the main reason, I'm not sure. But like I've told you, this is the time for Texans to make their state strong and great and orderly. I was thinking of that too." He threw her a shy grin. " Maybe my ideals weren't exactly responsible for me busting over the line though. It'd be pretty hard for me to separate my thoughts about you from what I believe in otherwise." His grin lingered and she smiled in response to it.

" Do you know, Clint; I think you're right. I think this really is the time of the Texan."

She gazed fully at him, seeing something she had never seen before; seeing a depth she had not suspected. There was, for example, a strong streak of fatalism in him; a conviction of personal destiny too strong for any other emotion to ever overcome—even love. He was a man who would live out his life-span forcing the future to emerge early and bow to his will. She remembered, from his kiss, that his temper was savage and unbending. Things which would appear minutely important to other men—the men she had known in the East—he would shrug aside as unimportant. He had been forged and toughened by frontier existence; environment had made him older in many ways than his years, and it was this, she now saw, which made him so taciturn at times, so dedicated to the things he believed in that he could not change. That, she saw very clearly, was why he would never go East with her. It was a revelation which left her a little breathless; she had never before seen so clearly nor deeply into another human being.

" I reckon we better go back," he said suddenly,

making as though to arise. " It'll be dark enough to make a run for it directly."

She accepted his hand, got upright and walked back towards the jumble of rocks with him. If a woman loved a man such as Clint Verrill she told herself, she could do only one of two things if she came from a different world from his; she could wrench herself away, leave him and never look back—or she could— would have to in fact—renounce everything of her earlier life and live in his world entirely. Because he was the kind of man he was there would be no compromise possible.

She was still thinking this when he stopped beside her boulder gazing down at her. " I'll send you some jerky."

" I have some, thanks," she said, studying the strong squareness of his face. " I have a canteen too."

His eyes twinkled. " Gallant bunch of boys I've got," he said, and reached out to catch her fingers, raise her hand and hold it briefly. " Get a little rest, Florence. I'll send you word in plenty of time." He let her hand go. " I'm sorry about this; it's going to be a wild ride. Just remember to stay close to whoever is riding with you."

Something craven stirred deep within her. She did not succeed at once in fighting it down. " Will it be very dangerous, Clint?"

" It'll be dangerous, Florence," he said, and started away through the murk and shadows.

From behind her a man's slouching silhouette spoke forward. " Biggest danger, ma'am, will be from horses stumblin' in the dark." The voice, conditioned by its owner to sound reassuring went on. " Mexicans can't hit nothin' in broad daylight so don't worry too much 'bout 'em hittin' anything much in the dark."

Clint found the possemen gathered together where he had left them an hour earlier. They watched his approach in silence and waited while he squatted among them. One of them offered his tobacco sack. Clint took it, worked up a brown-paper cigarette, lit up and blew forth a grey cloud.

" Anyone check the horses?" he asked, as a preliminary.

" They're saddled and ready," a wispy cowboy said, yawning behind his hand. " Everything's ready in fact."

The silence re-settled and drew out. " I thought sure Gollar'd have found Carl and brought him up by now," Clint said, worrying over missing Benton's posse and leaving it behind in the same position he and his own posse were now in.

There were a dozen divergent speculations possible here and the possemen, conscious of them all, said nothing of any of them. Perhaps Gollar had indeed located Benton's posse; possibly it had gone back to Travis for reinforcements. Possibly too, it was out there right now stalking the brigands. It was even plausible Benton and Gollar were waiting to reinforce Clint, surmising he would attempt a break-out after nightfall.

Clint looked at the tired, grey faces; there was not a one but that looked fully resolved to fight clear. He thought briefly as he had thought many times on other occasions that these were his kind of men. He smoked on in silence until a grizzled, older Texan spoke up.

"I been thinking," this man said drawlingly. "Durin' the war we used to find ourselves in pickles like this every once't in a while. Dang near always outnumbered too. We used to send a few fellers forward to slip up on the enemy, toss a fistful of ca'tridges into his fire and beat it. It never failed to give the rest o' the boys time to get away."

Someone chuckled, evidently envisaging the consternation such a ruse would cause among the Mexicans.

Clint smiled too, but he vetoed the proposition on grounds that, being surrounded as they were, any tardy riders would surely be caught before they caught up.

The silence settled again.

Clint was considering the possibility of Mexican constabulary troops being out there in the night somewhere, waiting. It was possible, he knew. He also knew from the faces around him that he had not originated this notion. "Well," he said eventually, pushing out the cigarette. "I reckon there's just one way to find out whether or not we're going to get out of this alive . . ." He arose. Around him men came silently up off the ground. "How many boys are still out in the rocks?" he asked.

The grizzled older man said : "Eight. I'll fetch 'em and meet you at the horses." He did not wait for Clint to speak but faded out in the darkness.

Clint sent another man to bring Florence and her

guards then led the balance of his party to where the horses were drowsing under saddle. As he and the others came up a shadow moved forward toward them out of pitch darkness.

"Ready?" A boyish voice asked, and when Clint nodded the youth turned immediately back into the underbrush to kneel and buckle on his spurs.

The men got their horses and stood loosely waiting. Florence came up with three men. She paused for a moment beside Clint then went on, led to the horse she would share with a lithe, tousle-headed cowboy, by her companions.

Men filtered out of the tree- and boulder-shadows, among them the older, grizzled rangeman. He nodded at Clint and continued on past. The Texan who had withstood that attack from the east side of their surround with the sheriff halted, grounded his carbine and said : " I did a little nosing around counting cookin' fires. Seems to me they got us plumb cut off to the north and west, Sheriff. I figure they don't want to see us get a run for the border."

" How about the south and east?"

" T'the east they got a couple dozen fires but to the south there aren't more'n six or eight." The cowboy paused. " 'Course; they'd like to have us head south deeper into Mexico because we'd have to work our stock pretty hard to get around them to the west and cut north toward the line. But I don't think we've got much choice. We got to head south."

" We've got to save the horses," Clint said. " We've got to try and slip past them without being seen. We'll walk the horses as long as we can. When we have to run, keep closed up and together. We won't be able to go back for anyone."

The men stood stone-like, listening and awaiting the order to mount. Clint was very conscious of Florence's gaze.

"Ride easy, boys," he concluded, turning to mount. "They'll have men out there with their ears to the ground. They can't hear a walking horse until he's close enough to be seen, but they can sure hear a running horse a mile off." He swung up. "Let's go."

Not a word was spoken. The Texans drifted shadow-like through the darkness. Occasionally a shod hoof struck granite and sparks flew. Saddles squeaked; there was the rustle of rubbing *rosaderos* and the soft jangle of rein-chains, but none of these sounds carried far although to the posseman they sounded loud enough to rouse the dead.

The land ahead, Clint recalled, sloped away southerly between two gentle rises. He knew, even before they came to the edge of their *pedregal* stronghold, that the wily brigand leader would have stationed men between the badlands and the southern plains athwart their escape route. Nor was he wrong; the little Mexican cooking-fires were visible even before he left the last pine-shelter to rein up studying the landfall ahead.

Beside him a man said hissingly : "Got to go west or east around them ridges, Sheriff. We'll never get down that little valley 'thout rousin' 'em."

Behind Clint several men muttered and a horse

stamped a foot. The latter sound brought an indignant admonition from someone farther back and an apologetic retort from the man whose mount had made the sound.

Beyond the final fringe of trees the sky shone darkly soft and cool. As yet the moon had not risen, which prompted Clint to think that at least in the lesser details his Texans were at least fortunate this night.

Chapter Six

CLINT DISMOUNTED, HELD forth the reins to his horse and said to the foremost men : " Stay here."

He went cautiously forward through the hushed night seeking to ascertain for himself how many brigands were at the campfire on ahead, and more important, if, should he elect to slip past them, there were other Mexicans farther down the land.

He did not anticipate discovery because he bore westerly as far as the swelling shoulder of the nearest rise and climbed quietly upwards to the ridge. Southerly, he saw with a sinking sensation, and well hidden from normal vision by the very rise he stood upon, were no less than a hundred and fifty fire-lights. Soldiers, he told himself, and bent a long appraising stare upon the pattern of flickering light. He remained atop the ridge for perhaps twenty minutes, picking his route, then started back.

The Mexicans were indeed clever. They had deliberately given the impression that they wished for him to head south. Obviously, with a route army camped beyond the hillock, he and his posse would not have seen it until they were past the brigands. After that, caught between two fires, his Texans would be cut to pieces and if any escaped they would have to continue on southward, there to be overtaken and butchered at leisure by their foemen.

He got back to his men, mounted, and without speaking flagged them onward striking out, not southerly as they expected, but south and west around the strong bulge of the nearest hill. There was, thanks to the hill itself, a very narrow corridor between the route army and the brigand camps, both on the prairie and both therefore bisected by the hill. It was, he knew fully, a very thin chance, almost a forlorn one, but it had to be taken and it was, after all, a chance.

Riding slowly, head up and alert to every sound and shadow, each faint echo of the riders behind him and of the coolness through which they were making their careful way, Clint was unconscious of the night-scent; the fragrance of pine-sap and vegetation. He was conscious instead of this ebb-hour of the night when weariness let a man's vitality run out and his thoughts turn nearly listless. He felt within himself scarcely any push at all; only the will to go on slowly, expecting to face a blinding orange muzzle-blast each hundred feet and not elated when none came.

Time passed, the *pedregal* was lost somewhere behind them and the hillock also fell away, its rounded fullness cutting a big chunk out of the easterly horizon. Occasionally a man's rough whisper carried forward but usually there was only silence; the kind of stillness which had no counterpart in everyday existence; the hush of withheld breath, of straining ears and searching eyes; not the silence of fear exactly but certainly the silence of dread and apprehension.

Clint stopped after an hour of steady riding. He got down, pressed his ear to the ground, got up and stepped back across the saddle and looked for a long moment backwards. Visible now to them all were the pin-pricks of quivering light where the route army was encamped. Someone, farther back in the posse, let off a discreet curse. Closer to Clint a man said : " Doggone; they put that little hill between us and them on purpose, figurin' we'd ride due south." When Clint remained silent the Texan said : " You seen 'em from the hill-top; correct?"

" Correct, pardner. Maybe we can out-shoot and out-fight 'em," Clint said. " But don't ever make the mistake of thinking all the brains are north of the border."

The man would have prolonged the conversation but Clint cut him off and reining forward, moved ahead with brigand fires visible on their right stretching in a miles-long arc around the *pedregal*-country they had vacated, scimitar-like and heaviest to the north.

There were now only occasional trees, their solid black shapes looming darkly at random with here and there a ravine or a brush-clump hummock building up deeper shadows against the skyline. Here too, the narrow corridor of escape pinched down still more with Mexican campfires coming close again, no longer

H

held apart by the hillock's long-spending, sloping flank.

Somewhere off in the darkness came the lilting, sad sound of a Mexican singing to the accompaniment of a guitar. Another time the Texans would have enjoyed listening; now, they used the sound only as a gauge to ascertain how near their closest enemies were.

Too close, Clint decided, and began angling a little more to the south fearful that some visiting rider or zealous picket would stumble onto his band, and reconciling himself to fleeing pell-mell westerly if such an event occurred.

A quarter hour passed; a half hour. They were nearing an area where the brigand campfires choked down forming a very narrow passageway. Beyond, where the little cooking-fires were farther apart and more southerly or northerly but in any case farther apart, lay escape. Clint chose his course and leaned from the saddle to whisper to the man beside him.

" Pass the word along : string out, be as quiet as possible and . . ." He paused, hearing far back a sudden beating of riders; the quick, hard calls of men to one another, and twisted in the saddle.

From near the end of the line a Texan spoke forward. " They're coming," he called out. " Those prisoners we left back there got loose and spread the alarm."

Clint shortened his reins and looked swiftly ahead. Evidently the brigands up ahead had not as yet heard the distant tumult. But again, as Clint was shaping words, came an interruption. This time to the north.

It was a sudden, explosive burst of gunfire. Now the Mexicans on ahead came to life; cries rang through the night; horse's hoofs thudded as men sprang to saddle. The moon, beginning to rise, caught and held ghostly shapes milling excitedly in the near distance.

Clint waited no longer. "Guns!" He yelled, setting his mount into a forward lunge, drawing and firing at the Mexicans, causing those nearest to him, already confused, to haul up in purest astonishment, stare fleetingly at the oncoming Texans then whirl away with shouts of alarm and panic.

Orange flashes cut hard against the darkness and on every side was the sound of running horses. Clint's attack had sparked a rout that did not end with the brigands immediately before his band of hard-riding Texans, but spread through the darkness to infect the more distant raiders with panic. Cries of fear filled the night. There was considerable wild firing too, as the brigands sprang astride and fled off into the night.

Farther back, however, was the solid sound of many oncoming riders, and Clint recognised in this the real peril. Deciding that the earlier eruption of gunfire to the north might have been made by Benton's posse, and recognising that whether this was true or not it was no longer possible for his posse to slip away southward, he swung with an upflung arm northerly, cutting wide around the nearest fires, leading his Texans toward the greatest number of Mexicans deliberately, for the elemental reason that he knew, in the condition of their horses and the numbers of their foemen, only this most desperate of chances might succeed. But even as he rode through the darkness he privately held very little hope.

In the confusion and gunfire his party swept forward fully a mile before they could distinguish that on ahead the firing was steady and deliberate. Somewhere ahead, then, lay friends. Riding by sound, racing down the night past startled Mexicans who did not fire at once because they incorrectly assumed the speeding body of horsemen were their friends, the Texans cleared no less than thirty brigand bivouacs.

They covered the second mile with bedlam around them. Far back a trumpeter's bugling indicated that the mass of riders they had heard were constabulary troopers from south of the hillock.

As long as their animals held up, Clint surmised they had little to fear from the soldiers because they had a lead of at least one mile. Then he sighted the darting flashes of gunfire to his right where the fight was raging and kept on northward until he was well past the site. There he drew down and finally halted. When his men swirled up he called to the nearest Texan : " The border is about two miles north from here. Take a couple of men and escort Miss Berry back to Travis."

Florence came up too. She started to protest but Clint was turning away, spinning his horse around to study the raging battle. There were, he saw at once, two clearly defined battle lines, and the battlers to the north while considerably less in numbers than their enemies, were nonetheless pressing the fight with angry vigour. Leading out at a slow walk, heading for the fight with caution uppermost, he determined when close enough that the northerly men were not Mexicans. It was obvious from the sharper, clearer ' crack ' of their guns. He was sure he had found Carl Benton's posse—and he had, but that was not all he had found.

The first man he saw when coming down behind the embattled Texans was Bruce Gollar. The dark-visaged rangeman was kneeling behind a dead horse punching cartridges into his carbine. Clint dismounted and called for horse-holders. When his men were converging on him afoot he sent their mounts back a safe distance and went swiftly forward. Gollar saw them coming and whirled. The sheriff called out swiftly identifying himself. Gollar continued to stand rocklike and wary until he could make out the advancing Texans, then he grinned a tight, wolfish grin, and said : " Nice to see you fellers are still alive."

" What the hell happened to you?" A Texan demanded.

Gollar got up and walked back a short ways. There, he turned a long stare southward towards the battle and for a moment he was silent, then he said : " I found Carl. He had stopped at the line and was waiting for us to come back. He wasn't exactly eager to cross over until he knew he had to. I convinced him." Gollar shrugged. " By the time we got down here the pepper-bellies were thicker'n flies around your stronghold. We figured to wait until night fall then slip through to you. The trouble was—those cussed Mexicans had rounded up an army from somewhere and their scouts found us." Another shrug. " You can guess the rest. We ran for it and dang near trampled the very same herd of brigands you'd routed. Since then we've been tryin' to slip around them in the dark." Gollar flagged southward toward the battle with his carbine. "That's the result. They doggone near trapped us too, and we got to fight our way out now." He looked up at Clint. "How far south is that army of 'em?"

"Not very far," the sheriff told him. "We had about a two-mile lead, Bruce, but they're coming up fast."

A listening posseman who was watching the fight south of them, said in a puzzled way : "I didn't know Benton had so many men."

"He didn't have," Gollar replied. "While he was waitin' he sent word back to Welker. Half those fellers down there are Welker's possemen."

Clint asked where Johnny and Carl Benton were. Bruce offered to go with him in search of them. All the Texans started forward and as soon as they were near the battle Clint's possemen split off to join the fight.

Welker and Carl Benton were in the centre of their line. Benton, whisker-stubbled and red-eyed, got up stiffly and joined Welker and the sheriff in a parley. He was angry and uncontrollable. "We got to break this off and get out of here," he told the other two leaders.

Welker, less perturbed, said he thought it would be a good idea if they finished what they had started by cleaning up the entire border country. Clint told them of the oncoming army. This sobered Johnny Welker.

" Then let's fall back," he said, and waited for Clint, whom they both tacitly acknowledged as leader, to speak.

" Pass the word along," Clint said. " Have your horses brought up. We'll have to move fast. I don't think the brigands will do more'n skulk along and snipe at us, but when that route army gets up here things will get pretty hot." He nodded. " Go on; I'll get my boys. They'll act as rearguard for the others. Let's go."

The withdrawal was carried out with the efficiency of a seasoned army and as Clint had expected, the brigands were not anxious to press on after the Texans. Clint's men formed a thin, elongated line between the posse's main body and their enemies, holding back the more daring Mexicans with brisk gunfire.

Clint, on the left of his line, heard someone calling his name in the night and went toward the voice. It was Welker. " I think we're going to make it," the young cowboy told him, " but from up where Carl's boys are I could see a big mounted party filtering up behind the brigands."

" That," Clint said with conviction, " will be the Mex army." Recalling their numbers he added : " Go tell Carl to make a run for the border. We don't stand a chance against those soldiers, there are too many of them."

Welker rode off northward in a long lope and moments later, as the Mexican fire began to swell significantly, Clint noticed that the distance between his line and the nearest Texans on ahead, was perceptibly widening. He shouted at the men closest to him, urging them to ride for it and to pass the word along.

The firing dwindled and what had been a raging battle became now a grim race northward. Occasional gunflashes shattered the darkness, but more numerous now than the reports of weapons was the solid thunder of running horses.

For an hour this running battle continued, then Clint's possemen began to lag. He knew what the trouble was and went in search of Welker and Benton. They were riding together and slowed a little as he came abreast of them.

" Our horses are giving out. They've had the worst of it for twenty-four hours and can't keep up much longer." He waved ahead. " You fellows keep going. I'll stay with my crew and those of us who can get away later will head for Travis."

Welker ground out a curse. He faced Benton. " You go on," he yelled over the swelling crash of increasing gunfire. " I'll stay here with Clint."

The massive blacksmith growled something in a low and incomprehensible tone and flung up his carbine-arm. Around him the riders slowed, holding their fire and looking over where he and the sheriff were riding.

" Clint's horses are played out," the blacksmith bawled. " He wants us to go on without him. Any of you that want to head out keep going. The rest—"

A great shout went up and without awaiting orders the Texans whirled about and went plunging back over the ground they had just traversed. Now the gunfire rose to a crescendo and south of them rose the dimly-heard cries of startled Mexicans.

Struck hard by the Texans, Mexicans, soldiers and brigands alike, were bowled over, shot down, and routed. The foremost riders fought to get clear of their savage attackers. Over their cries of consternation rose the Rebel Yell; that keening, terrifying howl of Confederate fighting men; it did perhaps as much as anything to demoralise the swarthy horsemen from south of the border and the triumph which had nearly rested with the Mexicans was wrenched away so suddenly that even the soldiers turned and fled for dear life.

Clint had the Texans recalled. He wanted to conserve horseflesh and regroup the scattered possemen. It took some time for all the Texans to be gathered together again; many of them, even when the firing died out completely for a time, were indignant; they wanted to finish whipping both brigands and soldiers.

Into the period of those silent moments Carl Benton ordered the men to cool-out their sweaty horses and check their guns. This latter matter, more than Clint's reasoning with them, had a sobering effect upon the Texans. They had not until then taken inventory of their ammunition. Now, they found very little left.

Clint was in the act of dismounting when a Texan jogged up and said : " Sheriff; they're comin' after us again. It's them cussed soldiers. They got re-organised and—"

" We can't stay here," Carl Benton said explosively. " There's nothing but open country in every direction."

"No," Johnny Welker interrupted to say. "Westerly there's some broken country; some ravines and rocks."

Clint re-mounted. "Lead out," he told the cowboy. "And save the horses."

The men got back astride and followed Johnny Welker grimly. Clint detailed another rearguard, but for nearly an hour they saw no Mexicans. Occasionally, far back, a gunshot sounded, but these sounds only apprised the Texans of the general location of the enemy, and indicated that they were skirmishing forward seeking to re-establish contact. It was, Clint thought, a favourable night after all; the Mexicans could not hear walking horses and what light the lopsided old moon gave was insufficient for their enemies to find them without hard riding; something they could no longer indulge in for the identical reason the Texans couldn't either; their horses were winded.

Clint came abreast of Welker. On Johnny's right rode Carl Benton and Bruce Gollar. Both were grimly silent and intent upon reaching the cover Welker had assured them lay ahead through the darkness.

"How much farther?" Sheriff Verrill asked the cowboy.

"Not far," Welker said without looking around, and abruptly his face cleared. "There; on ahead to the right."

This was not as protective a locality as the countryside Clint had led his posse out of several hours earlier but no one said so for the basic reason that any kind of covert, even chaparral, shallow ravines, a few gnarled junipers, and a scattering of crumbling flagstone was better than the barren prairie they had just come over.

"Get to cover!" Benton bellowed, and the Texan spurred past him, eager to obey.

Clint was studying the sky when Johnny Welker said : "Let me have your horse. We're sending them farther back."

As the sheriff got down he muttered : "It's better than midnight, Johnny. I believe some of the raiders will call it quits."

"They better," the rangeman exclaimed, cocking his head to listen. "Because after a couple more go-rounds with 'em we're goin' to be afoot in more than one way, Clint. I got fourteen carbine ca'tridges left and seven for my hand-gun. 'Don't believe the others are in any better shape."

A gunshot sounded in the east. "Take cover," Clint ordered the cowboy. "Pass the word to conserve bullets."

Welker bent a hard look at the sheriff. "Pretty hard to do that when you're bein' shot at," he said caustically, and walked away with Clint's horse.

Carl Benton came forward out of the night, stopped beside Clint and listened. Finally he said : "They're getting close, Sheriff." He paused briefly, drew back a breath and spoke again. "We got six wounded men. Four of 'em pretty bad."

"Can they ride?"

"Yes. At least they've managed to this far."

"Then go ask them if they want to stay here or go on up to Travis. If they want to go on, send three or four men with 'em."

Benton scowled. " We need every man," he said shortly. " Accordin' to my figures we got about ninety boys—countin' everyone; and those brigands got no less than a thousand, countin' those Mex soldiers. Maybe a couple thousand for all we know." He stopped, watching Clint. " You still want to send a few back with the wounded?"

" Yeah. Make it fast, Carl. They're coming up fast now."

Benton departed muttering under his breath and Clint walked forward for several hundred feet listening to the approaching riders, trying to get some idea whether all of them were coming up or whether most of them had turned back.

It did not sound as though there were any thousand horsemen out there. In fact it sounded like no more than fifty or sixty, although he surmised these might be simply the advance element. Of one thing he was certain; the Mexicans were not hurrying. They slowed even as he listened, and several of them called back and forth. Obviously, with the first taste of near-victory and subsequent rout very fresh in their minds, they were beginning to cool a little.

He heard one unseen rider say in Spanish that the Texans could not be far ahead. Another agreed with this and warned against a trap of some kind; perhaps an ambush. This suggestion slowed them still more. Finally they halted altogether, milled around talking, and ultimately sent forward a pair of scouts. Clint hurried back where Carl Benton was, related what he had heard and directed that word be passed for no one to fire or make any unnecessary noise. He then took Johnny Welker and slipped forward again, halting often and crouching low to sky-line the countryside for movement.

They located the Mexican riders in this fashion and remained close to the ground watching their progress forward with the skyline behind them. When Clint was sure of their course he touched Johnny lightly and they glided noiselessly to a point where the scouts would pass. Here, they lay flat, both with his short-gun palmed, waiting.

One of the scouts drew up squinting ahead. In Spanish he told his companion he thought there was something on ahead. The second scout, less timorous, answered scornfully that it was a juniper tree. The first man moved again, but with obvious reluctance, and finally he said : " I think we should go back. *Tejanos* are formidable marksmen."

The second Mexican halted, swore, and spat. His expectoration struck the ground less than ten feet from where Clint was lying prone, partially hidden by a struggling little chaparral bush. " I think," this man said in the same contemptuous tone, " that you are a coward. Look you; there are no more than a few of them and we are many. Now come on; they can't be much farther onward."

" They aren't," Clint said, arising with his hand-gun bearing unwaveringly upon the Mexican's chest. " They are very close, in fact—all around you. Now get down off that horse and if either of you yell I'll kill you!"

The timorous brigand clambered down immediately but his companion did not move until Johnny Welker rose up, grabbed his belt and flung him bodily to the ground, stood over him with his pistol less than a foot from the scout's face and said : " Go ahead; warn the others." He cocked the gun.

The Mexican said hoarsely : " No, *Señor*. I won't yell."

" Can't yell," Welker said, moving back so the Mexican could arise. " Too scairt to yell is what you mean."

When the horses had been secured by Welker, Sheriff Verrill drove the scouts along ahead of him as far as the juniper tree where Gollar and Carl Benton were waiting. There, Clint interrogated the Mexican who could speak English while his timorous companion nearly fainted as the rough, grim-faced Texans crowded up glaring balefully at him.

" Are the soldiers still coming?" the Sheriff asked, and the perspiring Mexican, no longer full of bravado with all those merciless eyes boring into him, licked his lips and nodded.

" *Si*. Yes, *Señor jefe*. It is their idea to capture what of you they do not wish to kill and march you in chains to the capital."

Around the Mexicans the possemen growled among themselves until Carl Benton turned a frowning, disapproving look upon them. The timorous Mexican was visibly shaking now.

" You two were with the raiders who had the girl?" Clint asked, and got another nod.

"*Si, Señor;* we are of that band. But we did not mean to—"

"And is your leader out there too?"

"Yes, *Señor.*"

"With those men who rode up here with you?"

"No, *Señor.* He wished to stay back and confer with the *soldados;* with their *teniente.*"

Johnny Welker smiled bleakly. "Seems to me he's never up where the fighting is," he said to the Mexican. "What kind of a *jefe* have you got anyway?"

The Mexican shrugged, preferring to say nothing to this whipcord-tough, dark-skinned man with the deadly eyes lest he say the wrong thing and be killed for tactlessness. He looked instead at Clint, refusing even to trade gazes with the massive, squat man beside the sheriff or the crowding, fierce faces over the sheriff's shoulder. He ignored his compatriot completely.

"*Señor,*" he said, when Clint did not speak at once. "They are going to surround you. You cannot win because they are too many. I tell you this in exchange for my life—you must waste no more time. They will all be up here soon."

Before Clint could reply a Texan said firmly: "It might slow 'em down a mite if they found these two hangin' from a tree limb, Sheriff."

There were mutters of approval and among the voices were Bruce Gollar's and Johnny Welker's. Clint did not heed the men but regarded the Mexican steadily. "Tell me," he said, conversationally. "Did your *jefe* mean to turn the *gringa* girl loose?"

The Mexican answered without hesitation. " No, *Señor,* he did not. He said a woman so pretty as that one should not remain behind for only *Tejanos* to enjoy." Fresh growls diverted the Mexican. He licked his lips again before finishing. " He said he would keep her for himself and perhaps later, he would turn her loose." The man's shoulders rose and fell in a typically Mexican gesture. " It was not for us to argue, *jefe.* You will understand that. But some of us feared such an affair as what came to pass would follow if he kept her— and *volgame Dios*—it did !"

" We're wasting time," Carl Benton broke in to say. " His friends out there aren't going to sit around all night, Clint."

The sheriff nodded. " Have the horses brought up," he said without looking away from the prisoner, and when Benton started to protest that they could flee no further because the animals were exhausted and also because there was no better place to make a stand, Clint said again : " Bring up the horses," but this time he added : " We're not going to run." To the Mexican he directed a final question : " Do you want to figure in our capture, *hombre?*"

" Not greatly," the Mexican answered, looking squarely into Clint's face.

" Why not?"

Another shrug. " You might have killed me. You had the right, but you did not. A man thinks of things like that, *Señor.*"

Clint stood a moment in thought, then gestured to Johnny Welker. " Keep them under guard. Take them out a ways and when I whistle turn them loose."

"Afoot?" Welker inquired, obviously thinking of the price the Mexican mounts would bring.

Clint's eyes twinkled. "Afoot," he said, and, taking Bruce Gollar's arm he walked away.

When the horses came up Clint, Bruce and the sheriff had a brief conversation, then scattered among the men. After that there was considerable activity among the possemen for perhaps half an hour, then Clint held another short parley with Welker and Benton, left them to walk out a ways and whistle. Within moments Johnny Welker came trotting back.

"'Turned 'em loose," he said, and waited.

"Get aboard, Johnny. We're going to make a short retreat."

The Texans rode slowly to the west and Johnny Welker did not notice at once that Clint had accompanied them only part way, then had handed his reins to another posseman and had trotted back on foot. By the time Welker located Carl Benton to ask what was happening, there came into the darkness some ragged gunfire back where the posseman had been and Johnny stopped short of where Benton sat, to listen and screw up his face in puzzlement. Around him the other men were also listening, but their expressions were for the most part anticipatory.

Clint found the thin skirmish line of Texans where they had been left. He took his place among them as the Mexicans, strongly reinforced again, began advancing and firing. Neither side had anything to shoot

I

at but muzzle-blasts for several minutes. When Clint saw the first ragged line of dark riders emerge from the night he let off a wail of panic, turned and fled. Around him the other Texans followed his example. The Mexicans, instantly heartened, broke over into a gallop shouting to those behind them that they had the Texans on foot and in headlong flight. Immediately the late hour rang with shots, shouts, and the thunder of straining horses.

Clint ran until his lungs ached, then stopped, turned about and knelt down. Around him the possemen also went low upon the earth, guns up and mouths open to suck in badly-needed air. They were as still as men could be, straining with expressions of fascination as the vague, swaying dark wave of riders came on.

Then it happened.

The first rank of horsemen struck the ropes Clint's Texans had tied hard and fast together and strung north and south for nearly a quarter of a mile. One second the brigands and soldiers were racing exultantly forward and the next second horses were upended, men were crying out in astonishment, in fear and terror and were pinwheeling through the air.

It was not possible for the crowding riders to haul up in time; behind them the forward pressure was too great; they continued to ride into the taut-stretched lariats until the writhing, struggling mass of horses and men completely covered an area of no less than ten acres.

Clint had to shout twice to his men to draw their attention away from the wreckage and lead them back where their companions were impatiently waiting.

"What happened?" Johnny Welker shouted, as Clint sprinted up and met the man who had his horse.

The sheriff did not reply but an older, fiercely grinning Texan said simply: "They tripped. Dangest sight I ever seen. Must of been three, four hundred of 'em piling over into each other."

Johnny's face cleared swiftly. He leaned from the saddle to peer around him at the saddle-swells of his companions. Very, very few of them still had lariats hanging there. "That" he said to no one in particular. "Hey, Clint; you just had to keep tryin' that stunt until it worked, didn't you?"

Bruce Gollar was arguing with Carl Benton when Clint came up and the blacksmith looked pained. "He wants to go down there and pile into 'em," Benton said to the sheriff. "Danged fool; just because we tricked 'em he thinks we can capture the whole herd of 'em."

"And if we captured them?" Clint asked the cowboy. "What'd we do with them?"

"Well . . ."

"Yeah," said Clint dryly. "Now let's get out of here. They're a long way from whipped but we've bought a little time and we badly need it."

The Texans continued riding westward. Their mounts had recovered their wind but they were still a long way from being recovered from their recent exertions. Clint was counting now on their ability to make good their withdrawal at a slow gait, which, he thought, would give them a slight edge over their enemies. He was counting on the fact that the irate Mexicans would need at least half an hour and maybe longer, to disentangle themselves, re-form, and continue the chase.

Chapter Seven

BUT CLINT HAD not counted on the craftiness of the brigand leader. The chieftain had kept his men back and it had been mostly soldiers who were unseated by the stretched lariats. While they halted long enough to care for their injured, catch loose horses and re-organise their companies, the outlaw chieftain led his men out around them and onward after the Texans. He was coldly determined to kill or capture every *norteamericano*. He had been made a fool of; he had been routed and forced to call for help. These things would support the ridicule of his enemies and no Mexican marauder of his stature was without enemies. Furthermore, once a brigand chieftain was made a laughing-stock he had difficulty recruiting men which meant the end of his career, and sometimes even of life itself.

Now, *el jefe* led his men resolutely down the night with an abandon which was contrary to his wily nature. He did not care whether he blundered into his enemies or not as long as he came up within firing range of them.

Clint, who might have suspected these things had

he been less concerned with his own problems, was concentrating on covering as much ground as could safely be covered in the present condition of their horses, when Bruce Gollar came up from the rear.

" Clint; there's a herd of 'em behind us and they're movin' right along."

The sheriff called for Carl Benton. When the blacksmith came out of the darkness he told him what Gollar had said. Benton threw up his hands.

" We can't run another step." he exclaimed. " There might be one more mile of running in these animals. If we kill them . . ." He did not finish. He did not have to. If they lost their mounts and were set afoot the Mexicans could wipe them out to a man.

" We could do like we did before," Gollar interposed hopefully. " We could turn around and run 'em down."

" And be that much closer to those doggone soldiers again?" The blacksmith said indignantly. " Don't be a fool, Bruce."

Clint heard the faint sound of oncoming riders. They seemed to be riding forward from a southeasterly direction and not, as he had assumed, directly from their rear. By making a slight northerly angle his men could move out of their path. He did not, right then, think beyond this ruse except to realise that when the brigands passed on by they would be in front of his Texans.

" Pass the word," he said to the blacksmith and Bruce Gollar. " Swing north and be very quiet. The Mexicans will pass us."

Nearly a hundred hollow-eyed men and horses changed course riding stealthily northward. They did not stop until Clint drew up several miles farther on, then every man got down to stand by his horse's head to prevent the animals from nickering when and if they smelt the Mexicans' mounts, and waited.

It was a long wait and a breathless one but Clint's ruse worked. The brigands passed by far to the south, faintly heard in the darkness. After they could no longer be heard a Texan said quietly : " Anyone want a piece of jerky?"

Carl Benton was for the first time this night, optimistic. " Let's head for home," he said, relief strong in his voice.

The men re-mounted and struck out behind Clint heading almost due north. They turned now, with the pressure gone, to looking after their wounded. Two men, both shot through the body, had been sent on ahead an hour earlier. There were another two injured riders but neither one had elected to leave. One had been pierced through the leg and rode now with a large piece of his shirt tied tightly over the wound. The other wounded man was a gory mess but actually his injury, except for the scar it would leave, was not serious : his left ear had been shot away.

Some of the men dismounted and trudged along leading their horses, in this fashion lightening the loads and helping the animals as much as possible.

The men began speaking among themselves, something they had had neither the time nor inclination to do before. Bruce Gollar told Johnny Welker he thought the Mexicans had learned a lesson. Johnny was not as concerned with this as he was with what would happen when the U.S. commandant at Fort Lincoln learned Texans had invaded Mexico, chased a brigand band and shot up a Mexican route army.

This thought was troubling Clint as well but he said nothing about it until Carl Benton said : " Clint; I been figuring. I think we'd best split up as soon as we're safe, and leave the country. I for one got no very strong hankering for spending the rest of my life in a federal calaboose."

When Clint continued silent the blacksmith twisted to look at him. " This'll cause a big smoke in Austin too," he continued. " It'll probably even make headlines in Washington—all over the country for that matter. A bunch of Texans bustin' down into Mexico and takin' on a Mex army." Benton wagged his head glumly and after a while spoke again, in a dull, flat tone. " A feller goes along mindin' his own business and livin' as honestly and decently as he can—then—in one night it's all wiped out. He's a fugitive; an outlaw."

Clint had no answer and offered none. He was remembering that brief period with Florence back in the *pedregal* and it was impossible not to feel slightly ironic over that, too. He did not shake the mood off until Bruce and Johnny, riding on ahead a quarter mile, came back to stop in front of him, their grimy, shadowed faces grim and resigned.

" Well," Welker said matter-of-factly. " We've gone about as far as we can go, Clint."

Benton squinted inquiringly. "Why?" he asked. "What's the matter?"

Johnny jerked his head to indicate the land behind him toward which they had been riding. "*Jefe*'s up ahead waiting."

"He can't be," the blacksmith exclaimed. "He passed us going west."

Gollar looked long at Carl Benton. "You know," he said, "I heard a feller say somethin' tonight that set me to thinking. He said all the brains aren't north of the border. He was plumb right, Carl. *Jefe*'s tracked us out some way; maybe he figured what we did—but anyway take my word for it—he's up ahead in the chaparral waitin' to cut us down when we ride up."

"You saw them?" asked the sheriff.

Welker nodded. "Yep. Heard 'em talking, then scouted 'em up on foot. They didn't see us but we sure saw them."

"Change course," Clint said wearily, "and no noise. We'll try heading east to go around them."

"Not east!" Benton said sharply. "The soldiers'll be east of us somewhere."

"They'll be south," Clint corrected him. "If they follow *jefe*'s band they'll ride south. *Jefe'll* know this too, don't think he won't, and he'll have most of his men strung out north and west thinking we won't dare risk going east or south for fear of running into the troops." He watched the blacksmith's grey face turn gloomy. "What else can we do, Carl?" he asked. "We can't run and we're not strong enough to put up

a fight. We don't have enough ammunition either."
He reined to his right. " Come on. Johnny; ride among
the men and explain what's happened. Bruce; go on
ahead and scout the way for us."

The bleak elation of moments before when the
Texans thought they were riding clear of disaster
turned now to a depth of bitterness and despair such as
they had not evidenced before, even when their
earlier dangers had seemed greater.

The hour was well advanced : men and animals
moved across the plain dumbly, horses listless, riders
deeply silent, strongly feeling a hopelessness that no
amount of talk would have alleviated, but still as
dangerous, as fully deadly as a rattlesnake; as resolved
to die, if they had to die, standing as their forefathers
had stood at the Alamo, ankle-deep in Mexican
blood.

Clint felt the marrow-deep tiredness of his body.
He was for the first time conscious of its aches and
bruises. Beside him massive Carl Benton slouched
along, carbine balanced across his lap. " I don't know
as it makes me feel any better," he told the sheriff,
" but those brigands must be as tired as we are and I
know their horses are as worn out as our critters are."

Clint, disinclined to talk, nevertheless felt an obliga-
tion to do so now. " We'll make it," he said quietly.

Benton looked around, his voice rising. " How?"

" Because we have to, Carl."

Something in the sheriff's voice went deep into
Benton; he rode a while longer in silence, then he
mumbled : " Yeah."

A half hour later Bruce Gollar met them on foot beside his horse. "There's a heavy brush thicket on ahead," he reported. "We can rest a spell there if you want to."

Clint nodded. "Lead out," he replied.

The thicket was deep and unfamiliar as Clint's men approached it and swung down. "Scouts out," the sheriff called, leaving it up to the men who the scouts would be, confident that without making certain, his Texans would fan out. "Bruce; make a sashay northward. We'll rest until you get back." As Gollar faded from sight Carl Benton came forward with Johnny Welker. He looked worried.

"Tell him," he ordered.

The cowboy spoke quietly. "*Jefe's* men are trailin' us on foot, Clint. I don't know whether they're doing it because it's the only way they can pick up our sign in the poor light or whether it's because their horses are done for—but anyway they're behind us about a mile."

"How many?"

"Pretty big bunch of 'em. About as many men as we've got I'd guess. I didn't get much of a look at 'em back there but I could hear 'em."

Carl Benton, watching the sheriff's face, said: "Now what?"

"Fight," the sheriff said shortly. "Let's go."

The Texans left their head-hung horses with a guard detail and followed Clint back the way they had come. There was very little cover and the moonlight struck slantingly now at this late hour, brightening the land in an oblique fashion.

"Quiet," Clint called. "Get down; don't fire until I do." He looked around at the lowering dark shapes. "Keep close to one another. Don't let them get in among us."

Benton and Johnny Welker shuffled over to stand beside the sheriff listening as he was doing. For a time none of them heard anything. In fact the blacksmith whispered hopefully to Welker: "You sure it wasn't night-shadows you saw?"

Welker extinguished Benton's hope in a short sentence. "Shadows don't speak Spanish."

As Johnny was finishing, the sheriff's hand struck his arm in quick warning. Out of the fraught stillness came a sound of spur rowels. Clint faded against the earth and around him his possemen did likewise, all blending with the gloom.

Clint saw a sudden faint streak of movement a hundred feet ahead of him; it came noiselessly closer then halted long enough for the sheriff to make out the rigid silhouette of a man, his head up and his body attuned to the stillness. He was sure he recognised *el jefe,* leader of the brigands, by the shape of his sombrero. An idea came to him as he watched the raider resume his stealthy advance. Drawing close to Carl Benton he whispered: "Stay here and remember—no shooting until I open up."

Benton moved his head to speak but the sheriff was already crawling away. Johnny Welker raised his head only high enough to watch. It was plain he wished to speak, but he lowered himself gently without surrendering to the urge.

Clint crawled to the left of the brigand chieftain without once looking away from him, and stopped moving only when *el jefe* also paused. The Mexican seemed to draw up, to stiffen slightly as though suddenly conscious of danger. Then he stalked forward again angling slightly to his left and holding up a hand to the men crowding up behind him, indicating for them to wait, to stay where they were. None of the other brigands seemed the least bit reluctant to obey and stopped. Some sank swiftly down upon the ground seeking to catch movement by skylining the countryside ahead. They saw nothing for the simple reason that no Texans were standing upright to be skylined.

El Jefe glided another twenty feet and stopped again. This time it was obvious to Clint that the Mexican more than sensed danger because he reached low, drew a wicked-bladed dagger from his boot-top and held it pointing forward, obviously thinking to kill silently when he located the man he knew was somewhere ahead of him.

Moving his arm an inch at a time Clint reached for his short-gun, gripped it in a sweat-slippery hand and very slowly, very silently, drew it from the holster and brought it forward. He raised up inches off the ground, got his toes dug in under him to spring upright when the time came, and watched the brigand leader until his eyes burnt from the effort.

El Jefe began his cat-footed advance again, moving directly toward Clint, and when the Texan knew discovery was imminent he sprang. The brigand saw him coming through the air almost at once and threw up one arm to ward off the hurtling body while he slashed outward with the knife-hand. Clint's gun-arm was swinging in a powerful short arc. He saw the knife for a fleeting second then felt his gun-barrel jolt with a solidness of steel hitting bone against the brigand leader's forearm. *El Jefe* reeled. He made no attempt to brace forward and the searing pain from his broken arm caused him to cry out thinly. Then Clint's gun-arm swung again in a high overhand movement and crunched through *el jefe's* sombrero into his skull. The brigand chieftain crumpled. There was a little soft rustle as his body flattened loosely upon the ground, but it was lost at once in a bedlam of shouts from his companions farther back and their nervous gunfire. Clint, instead of feeling triumphant over his narrow victory, pressed his body against the earth with a hard curse. He had hoped to kill his adversary silently and felt that he might have too, if the brigand had not cried out.

Spurts of dust jerked to life near him where Mexican bullets struck. He squirmed around and crawled hastily back towards his companions. For a time the Texans did not fire, for which he was thankful because he was between the lines, then he heard Carl Benton's bull-bass give the order and bullets sang overhead. He crawled faster.

A carbine barrel came over the ground to stop Sheriff Verrill still. Behind the sights was a savage pair of pale eyes. " Hold it," the sheriff gasped, and the Texan lowered his weapon, emitting a shaky sigh as he did so. He did not speak and neither did Clint. It had been a near thing.

Johnny Welker came up while Clint was brushing soil off his clothing. " Who was that yelled?" The cowboy demanded.

" That," the sheriff said with finality, " was *el jefe*."

" You got him?"

" I got him !"

Welker pondered this for a moment while around them gunfire swelled and flashed. " Do his lads know it yet?"

Clint turned toward the firing. " They'll find him," he told the cowboy.

" Then they'll break off and leave." Welker exclaimed with unconcealed exaltation.

The sheriff speared him with a hard stare. " Johnny; do you hear anything?" he asked.

" Sure. Gunfire."

" Listen harder," Clint ordered, and Welker knew at once what he meant. South of them was the unmistakable sound of many running horses. The soldiers were coming towards the increasing battle. He nodded and started away to join the others.

This, Clint told himself, would be the end of it. They had fought long and well but from this position they would be unable to retreat again. Their horses were no longer usable, their ammunition was nearly exhausted, the men were worn down and their enemies were swiftly fanning out all around them. He thought for just one moment of Florence; visualised her look of concern when last they had seen one another, then shook off the memory and forced himself around to face into the blossoming gunfire that winked with increasing brightness less than a thousand yards west of him.

Bruce Gollar came hurrying back towards the gunfire. When he located Clint he dropped down beside him and yelled : " They're all around us !"

" Shoot," Clint ordered, selecting a gunflash and firing at it.

The Texans battled grimly, doggedly, and mostly silently. Around them bullets whipped through chaparral and struck stone or dirt sending up geysers of dust. The Mexicans, scenting final victory, were both noisy and exultant. Their loudest yells were full of grisly prophecies and promises.

Carl Benton sought out the sheriff. He looked filthy, haggard and dishevelled, but strangely calm. " Had to tell you," he shouted over the crashing thunder of battle. " You did right, Clint, when you went over the line. 'Had to tell you that in case I don't get the chance later."

In the same loud tone Sheriff Verrill called out : " Thanks, Carl. And thanks for supporting me."

" One more thing, Clint. Whether we come out of this or not, I got a notion the Army'll start patrolling the border after this fight, so maybe, after all, we did what we all been thinkin' ought to be done—we cleaned up the south end of Texas."

Clint nodded in silence.

A Texan wearing a torn shirt crawled up breathlessly. " They got a doggone cannon," he yelled at

Clint. " I seen 'em bringing it up and shot the lead gun-horse. But that ain't going to stop 'em for long."

Clint faced the blacksmith. " Carl; go back with him. Take some men and keep them from firing that gun !"

The blacksmith bawled for men and started away after the ragged Texan. Around him, Clint saw the possemen watching; their faces, grey and dirty almost beyond recognition, were no longer tired appearing. He lowered himself against the earth again, faced forward in the darkness and searched for targets.

The fight was savagely prosecuted by the Mexicans but try as they might and for all their greater numbers they could neither force the Texans to give way nor slacken their fire. Overhead, where the moon was dropping low, diamond-like stars winked coldly and lower, hard against a horizon that held a very faint, brightening glimmer, rind-like, of pre-dawn, the land sloped outwards in a steady long dark silhouette. It was here that Clint caught a glimmer of movement, far out; so distant in fact that he at first attributed it to either the tiredness of his mind or the great distance. But as he watched he saw the movement fade out in an oncoming way, and at an interval, other similar movement appear over the skyline.

He stopped firing and concentrated on this phenomenon, thinking it must be reinforcements for the Mexicans although it was not approaching the field from the right direction for this unless the enemy was attempting a new maneouvre.

Ten minutes later he was sure that what he had seen

K

was horsemen and he alternated between desperate hope and crushing dread. Whoever the riders were, they were descending upon the battlefield in great numbers and they were moving swiftly. Except for the paling horizon he would never have discovered them at all. But in the end, whoever they were, he could spend little time in watching, for unexpectedly the Mexican gunfire was drowned out in the shattering roar of a fieldgun.

For a moment after this explosion the possemen slackened their fire, looking apprehensively over their shoulders. This was something the majority of them had not anticipated, although, if they had had more leisure to speculate upon the probability of artillery they surely would have come to think of it for the elemental reason that Mexican route armies were never without cannon and mountain howitzers.

While the lull lasted Clint used it to put his chin upon the ground and rummage the night for the black crowd of riders he had seen. They were no longer visible, having advanced too far down the land to be skylined any longer.

He considered ordering the men to crowd up close so as to present a solid wall against charging horsemen. In the end he decided that the newcomers would be unable to charge them successfully because of the chaparral and held his silence.

Gradually, the rifle and carbine fire swelled again and while Clint tensed, unconsciously waiting for the cannon to fire again, it never did. After a time he thought it likely that Benton had gotten close enough to discourage the gunners. This thought, though, was not followed by any great feeling of satisfaction; if the blacksmith and his possemen had gotten that close he was sure they had paid dearly in lives for their bravery.

At the height of the resumed firing a bugle sang out clearly over the din. At first Clint heard it without heeding it, then he started as the call came again, its urgent call fluting outward, echoless and compelling. He raised up recklessly daring to hope. As he did so an arm came up and roughly pushed him earthward. It was Johnny Welker's arm and his voice slashed through the noise.

" Keep down ! What you tryin' to do—get killed !"

" Johnny ! I've heard that bugle call before !"

" So've I," shouted the cowboy. " When the greasers were chasin' us !"

" *No!*" Clint yelled. " At Fort Lincoln ! Those are U.S. soldiers out there ! I saw them charge over the skyline a while back !"

Welker sat up suddenly, forgetting he had only a moment before admonished the sheriff against the same thing. He cocked his head northward straining to discern the bugle call which was being played over and over again, growing louder as the earth shook beneath him to the drumming of strongly charging horses. Finally, in a voice so awed and soft the sheriff did not hear it, he said : " You're right. Good Lord you're right . . ."

Out of the darkness a bullet came silently and pierced Johnny Welker's skull from back to front. He leaned gently forward and slid downwards, softly smiling.

"Johnny! Johnny!"

"Hey, Sheriff . . . !" It was Carl Benton, his mouth slack with relief and excitement.

"He's dead," Clint said, straightening up from Johnny Welker's side.

The blacksmith looked dumbly at the quiet form and knelt. His voice lost its hope and strength; in a solemn way he said: "It's soldiers from Fort Lincoln . . ."

Beyond where they knelt beside Johnny Welker the Mexican fire firmed up into volley-firing. In return the Texans raised their Rebel Yell and hastening forward, running crouched over and eager, came dozens of blue-uniformed shapes.

Five minutes later the slashing Texan gunfire had swelled to such an extent that the Mexicans could be heard yelling in alarm. Their firing became ragged; they were dropping back; many, unable to understand what had happened and suddenly, in the face of the increased deadliness of their foemen's fire, concerned only with preservation, flung aside their weapons and unashamedly fled.

Clint was roused from his position when Bruce Gollar came up leading a tall, fiercely moustached cavalry officer. "This here," the cowboy said, "is Captain Parker from Fort Lincoln, Clint. Captain: this here is Sheriff Clint Verrill of Travis, and this other feller is . . ." Gollar's voice trailed off into silence neglecting to complete the introduction of Carl Benton. He knelt beside dead Johnny Welker, peering into his face.

" Sheriff; we got word of your predicament this afternoon. I mean yesterday afternoon." A bullet clipped close and the officer winced, then squatted down. " I want you to order your men to cease firing."

Clint turned away, cupped his hands and yelled loudly : " Hold up, boys! Stop shooting!" He might as well have saved his breath; the Texans, even those closest who must have heard, did not lower their guns. The cavalry officer pondered this briefly then stood upright again.

" Just one thing to do," he said, not without bitter pleasure in his tone. " Charge those damfools! Bugler! Bugler! Hey, trumpeter; where are you man?" Several soldiers converged upon the officer. He snapped orders at them. " Mount the regiment! Bugler; wait two minutes then sound The Charge!"

When the cavalrymen were a-saddle Clint's Texans rose up around them. When that clear, fluting sound broke over everything else as the trumpeter sounded off, the Texans, afoot, so weary they staggered and so ragged they scarcely looked human, trotted along in their wake.

More courageous, less exhausted troops than the Mexicans would have flinched before that attack, and the Mexicans did not wait for their frantic officers to order them to flee; in their panic they over-ran their own bugler before he could blow Retreat, expedited by another curdling Rebel Yell from the oncoming Texans.

Clint and Carl Benton went forward as the cavalry-men came back, riding stiffly upright, some of their sabres blooded, all of their faces flushed and bleakly triumphant-looking in the brightening light of another day.

" Sheriff; a moment of your time please."

Clint halted, watched the officer dismount and hand his reins to an orderly. He had with him a small party of soldiers who were herding along two bedraggled Mexican officers.

" Sheriff; I have just been informed by Lieutenant Garcia here that he was repelling an invasion of Mexico by Texans. This is a very grave charge and I want your views on it."

Clint regarded the Mexican officer first, then the moustachioed cavalryman. There was something about the U.S. officer's clean uniform and well-fed face that irritated him.

" Believe what you like," he said, and started to turn away.

" *Sheriff!* If what I've been told is true, believe me, the Federal Government—"

" Oh hell," a growling voice interrupted to say flatly. " Listen, Gen'l; we got a right to protect ourselves, ain't we?"

Every eye turned to stare at the scarecrow of a posse-man who was standing there torn, bruised, bandaged, and calmly chewing a great cud of tobacco.

" Well; ain't we?"

" Certainly," the officer answered bristlingly.

" Well look-a-here, Gen'l. We—"

"Captain! Captain Parker!"

"All right; Captain then. Look-a-here Captain; you got any idea where you are?"

"What do you mean!" the Captain demanded sharply.

The scarecrow raised a lean arm pointing southward. "This here is Texas, Captain. We done crossed that silly line 'teen Mexico and the U.S. at midnight last night. We been fightin' for our cussed lives for near' five hours on U.S. soil against invadin' Mexican troops. Stick *that* in your pipe and smoke it!"

The gangling, ragged Texan raised his carbine, cradled it across one arm, spat copiously then turned with ludicrous dignity and stalked away. For a time after he had gone among the milling, loudly-talking soldiers the possemen did not speak. Then Clint, wanly smiling, said : "Well, Captain; how does it look to you now?"

The officer looked from Clint to Carl Benton and back to the sheriff again. "Is that true?" he asked. "Are we north of the border?"

"At least seven miles north," Clint said.

The officer's body sagged with relief. He gazed down at the Mexican officer. "Does that man speak any English?" he asked of the Mexican's guards.

"Yes sir, *Capitan*," the captive answered for himself. "I speak English."

"Then perhaps you will tell me," the U.S. officer asked coldly, "what you were doing, leading an invading Mexican army into the United States?"

The Mexican's eyes widened. His face blanched. He breathed something under his breath which none of them understood and fell silent.

" Well? I am asking, sir, for a full explanation !"

Clint, seeing fear, up like a banner in the Mexican's eyes and understanding his predicament—he would be executed on the spot as soon as the United States Government complained of his U.S. invasion—said quietly in Spanish, which he thought the U.S. officer did not understand : " *Amigo;* you had better tell him you were not invaded by Texans after all."

" Ai?" the Mexican said hopefully. " How is that, *Señor?*"

" You were simply pursuing Mexican brigands in the darkness, *Teniente* Garcia, and somehow—because it was such a miserably dark night, you inadvertently crossed into the United States."

Lieutenant Garcia's eyes lighted up; relief came over his face improving his colour. He blurted out what Clint had said; he rolled his eyes and gestured convincingly with his hands; he enlarged upon the story, then, faintly frowning, he looked at Clint and said in Spanish : " But *Señor*—the brigand leader will tell a different story."

" No; *teniente.* You see I killed him. I think, in fact, you had better tell the Mexican authorities the same story. When you take back the corpse of the brigand chieftain which I am prepared to assure the world you killed in combat yourself."

Again the Mexican lieutenant's face lit up; again he exploded into swiftly spoken English, explaining also

with great fidelity to improvised detail how he, Lieutenant Manuel Fidel Garcia y Fernandez, had person-
ally vanquished the terrible outlaw chieftain in hand-
to-hand combat.

The Fort Lincoln cavalry officer listened impassively
to the entire harangue, then turned aside and asked
his adjutant for casualty reports.

" None, sir," the junior officer stated briskly. " None
killed, none wounded."

" Fine. Have the men mounted and lined out. And
Adjutant; have the Texans helped. I think men who
have so bravely repelled what they mistakenly thought
was a Mexican invasion of the United States deserve
all the assistance we can offer them."

" Yes sir."

Clint turned as Carl Benton came up with their
mounts. He hauled himself into the saddle, unaware
that the cavalry officer's steady, unsmiling gaze was
fixed upon him. " See to the men," he told Benton.
" Hunt up Bruce . . . He can help."

As Clint reined away the U.S. officer turned, regarded the Mexican lieutenant for a silent long
moment, then said in faultless Spanish : " Look you,
teniente; I think it is as the *Tejano* told you. You
crossed the line after a Mexican brigand. You crossed
the line in the darkness unknowing where, exactly you
were. I think too so brave a man as the slayer of the
brigand leader will surely get a medal—if he does not
change his story. You understand?"

Lieutenant Garcia's astonishment faded as the captain continued to speak. When Parker concluded

Garcia was very faintly smiling. " Perhaps, *mi Capitan,*" he suggested, " it would be as well if the *Tejano* sheriff did not know you understood what he told me to say."

" It will be as well," Captain Parker agreed with a short nod. " It will be as well for you also, *teniente,* because if you say Texans invaded Mexico I shall be obliged to say that I found you north of the line invading Texas. In your country officers are shot for things such as that, are they not?"

Garcia did not reply to the question, he simply let one eyelid droop to cover the eye, touched his visor respectfully and said, " I will go at once with my men back to my own country if you will permit it."

" Permission granted, Lieutenant. Good luck and good-bye."

Clint and his possemen, riding apart from the Fort Lincoln troopers did not see the U.S. officer again that early morning. They did, however, meet a horde of anxious townsmen and cowboys heading south with Will Custer, and they were full of questions. Clint told Custer what had happened and referred him for additional information to the cavalry captain. Custer spurred on south to find the officer and after he had departed Clint smiled tiredly at Benton.

" One thing about Will," he said. " If he doesn't have much stomach for fighting, at least he has a nose for news."

The possemen arrived back in Travis shortly after sunup. A few of them went thirstily into saloons while others struck out for their homes or ranches. A small number went with Clint and Bruce Gollar to the undertaker's shed and left the only Texan killed outright in the entire battle : Johnny Welker. Afterwards, Sheriff Verrill went to the hotel, ordered a hot bath, languished in it for half an hour, then dressed in fresh clothing, went down to his office and waited for the storm to break.

It never did. Travis was alive with rumours and tall tales but Captain Parker and his troopers skirted wide of the town on their way northward to Fort Lincoln and even the Travis Town Council did not call for an explanation for the simple reason that Carl Benton told them that he thought Sheriff Verrill had done exactly what had needed doing for ten years, and if anyone wanted to argue the point he would meet them outside of town after nightfall with guns or bare fists.

Clint was not bothered, which was just as well, because he fell asleep at his desk in the office and did not awaken until nearly ten o'clock that night. When he did finally awaken though he sprang up as though shot, scooped up his hat and left the office in a rush.

Outside, another fragrant summer night was down and Travis, considerably more noisy than usual, was also too dark for the curious townsmen and cattle ranchers to catch sight of Sheriff Verrill as he hurried toward the hotel.

He was staring up the walkway toward the veranda without looking right or left when out of the murk a quiet voice reached forth to arrest him.

"I looked in at the office an hour ago, Sheriff. You were dead-to-the-world."

He turned and stopped. She was smiling up at him from a wicker chair. He went closer and reached out. She came to her feet gracefully, accepted his arm and they walked out into the night.

"I want to tell you something, Clint. I want you to understand—"

"Sure," he interrupted to say quietly. "I understand, Florence. You don't have to say it."

She stared up at him, then very slowly began shaking her head. "No; I don't think you understand at all, Clint. What I want to say is that—well—you have been right all along."

He stopped in mid-stride.

"Yes: you have been right. This *is* the time of the Texan. What you've done has proved it."

"Florence . . ."

"Please let me finish, Clint. You not only were quite right but I was very wrong. The East wasn't created without its pioneers either. I know that. And I also know that when a woman loves a man she belongs where he is—wherever that may be. That she is as necessary to his success in a raw country as in a settled country."

He continued to stare down into her eyes, his mouth closed with pressure, his jaw-muscles rippling faintly in the gloom.

"Clint: If you'll have me . . ."

He swept her into his arms; he pressed his mouth

to her lips with a powerful hunger and she returned the forcefulness of his kiss with a strength and a hunger of her own.

THE END

Lauran Paine who, under his own name and various pseudonyms has written over 900 books, was born in Duluth, Minnesota, a descendant of the Revolutionary War patriot and author, Thomas Paine. His family moved to California when he was at an early age and his apprenticeship as a Western writer came about through the years he spent in the livestock trade, rodeos, and even motion pictures where he served as an extra because of his expert horsemanship in several films starring movie cowboy Johnny Mack Brown. In the late 1930s, Paine trapped wild horses in Northern Arizona and even, for a time, worked as a professional farrier. Paine came to know the Old West through the eyes of many who had been born in the previous century and he learned that Western life had been very different from the way it was portrayed on the screen. "I knew men who had killed other men," he later recalled. "But they were the exceptions. Prior to and during the Depression, people were just too busy eking out an existence to indulge in Saturday-night brawls." He served in the U.S. Navy in the Second World War and began writing for Western pulp magazines following his discharge. It is interesting to note that all of his earliest novels (written under his own name and the pseudonym Mark Carrel) were published in the British market and he soon had as strong a following in that country as in the United States. Paine's Western fiction is characterized by strong plots, authenticity, an apparently effortless ability to construct situation and character, and a preference for building his stories upon a solid foundation of historical fact. *Adobe Empire* (1956), one of his best novels, is a fictionalized account of the last twenty years in the life of trader William Bent and, in an off-trail way, has a melancholy, bittersweet texture that is not easily forgotten. *Moon Prairie* (1950), first published in the United States in 1994, is a memorable story set during the mountain man period of the frontier. In later novels such as *The Homesteaders* (1986) or *The Open Range Men* (1990), he showed that the special magic and power of his stories and characters had only matured along with his basic themes of changing times, changing attitudes, learning from experience, respecting nature, and the yearning for a simpler, more moderate way of life. His most recent Western novels include *Tears of the Heart*, *Lockwood* and *The White Bird*.